PROTECTING THE DESERT PRINCESS

PROTECTING THE DESERT PRINCESS

BY

CAROL MARINELLI

DUDLEY LIBRARIES	
000000755372	
Askews & Holts	06-Apr-2015
	£13.99
HB	

First published in Great Britain 2014
by Mills & Boon, an imprint of Harlequin (UK) Limited,
Large Print edition 2015
Eton House, 18-24 Paradise Road,
Richmond, Surrey, TW9 1SR

© 2014 Carol Marinelli

ISBN: 978-0-263-25606-2

Printed and bound in Great Britain
by CPI Antony Rowe, Chippenham, Wiltshire

CHAPTER ONE

'PRINCESS LAYLA, ARE you excited to be…?'

Layla patiently waited as the little girl on her computer screen faltered while choosing her words. By video link Layla was being beamed into the classrooms of the girls and young women of Ishla. Each class took an hour and, by working hard, Layla managed to get to each classroom once a month. Here she encouraged the children to converse in English and to work harder on their schoolwork, and it was proving a huge success.

'Princess Layla.' The little girl tried again. 'Are you excited that you will travel to Australia with Prince Zahid and Princess Trinity on their honeymoon?'

At the word 'honeymoon' the class exploded into a fit of giggles and Layla did her best not to join in with them. This class consisted of ten-year-old girls and they were all terribly excited that the handsome Prince Zahid had married the English lady Trinity, and they were all only too happy to talk about weddings.

And honeymoons!

'Well done,' Layla said to the little girl when the laughter had died down. 'You asked your question beautifully. Yes, I am very excited that I shall be joining my brother and his bride in Sydney, Australia. Did you know that you are my final class before we leave on the royal plane tonight?'

Zahid and Trinity's wedding had been beautiful, and the whole of Ishla had joined in the celebrations, even though the shocking news had hit, just before the wedding, that Trinity was already pregnant.

Layla's rule was that so long as questions were politely asked she would answer as best she could. Some of the questions, though, about Trinity's pregnancy, had been more than awkward—and not just because the subject in Ishla was sensitive. Layla simply hadn't known the answers, and had begun to understand just how naïve she was.

Layla craved knowledge.

She had long dreamt of a world outside the palace walls.

Before Zahid had even known who his bride was he had agreed to allow Layla to accompany him on his honeymoon. As a future king Zahid could not be expected to entertain his wife all day, and of course it had been assumed that his bride would need a companion.

They were so deeply in love, though, that perhaps they would prefer to be holidaying alone—but there was no way Layla was going to give up her first and only trip out of Ishla.

Guilt gripped her.

Not because she might prove a bit of an imposition for a couple in love—instead the guilt was for what Layla was secretly planning to do when she got to Australia.

'Princess Layla, are you scared?' another little girl asked.

'A little.' Layla spoke a guarded version of her truth. 'After all, I have never been out of Ishla, and so I don't really know what to expect, but I am also very excited. It is going to be a huge adventure for me and I have been looking forward to it for a very long time.'

'Princess Layla…'

All hands were raised. Her students adored her. They always did their homework now, just for the chance to speak with their princess each month. There were a lot of questions, but Layla's father, King Fahid, wanted to speak with Layla before she left and so she brought things to a close.

'Now,' Layla said to the students, 'there is no more time for questions. Instead it is time for you all to wish me a safe journey.'

She smiled at their voices as they did just that.

'Will you miss us?' they asked.

Layla held up her finger and thumb and held them a small distance apart. 'This much,' she said. As they all moaned their protests Layla stretched out her arms as wide as she could reach. 'Or perhaps this much! All of you know that I will miss you to the moon and back.'

She would miss them very much, Layla thought a little while later, as she lay on her bed on her stomach, going through her computer and checking and rechecking details for the very last time.

Would her father even let her teach them again, after she—?

Layla halted her thought processes; she could not allow herself to think like that now. Whatever the consequences to her actions, Layla had long ago decided that she was prepared to bear them.

One week of freedom would be worth whatever punishment her father would serve out for her.

Layla was petrified about taking a taxi alone in Australia, but she had watched little clips on her computer over and over and was as certain as she could be that she knew what to do.

How she loved her computer!

King Fahid was getting older and, though no one in Ishla must know, he was seriously ill, so perhaps had not investigated Layla's teaching aid quite as thoroughly as he once would have. Fahid did not really understand the access to the world that the computer gave his daughter. Layla lived a very protected life and wasn't even allowed a phone—she had never seen a television.

The computer was to assist with her teaching. Fahid was pleased that his daughter was helping the young women of Ishla and that *finally* his rebel daughter seemed to be staying out of mischief's way.

Layla pulled up the page that she had been studying carefully for weeks now—ever since she had found out where the honeymoon was taking place.

There he was!

Layla smiled at his scowling, haughty face.

Mikael Romanov, Senior Counsel, was, according to everything she had read, an extremely successful barrister. According to the translation of his website, he was considered amongst the best criminal defence lawyers in Australia. Originally from Russia, he had studied law in Australia. Tough and ruthless, he attacked the prosecution on every point and all too often won.

Good, Layla thought. He would need to be tough and ruthless to deal with Zahid, and possibly even the King.

Layla typed in his name and read a translation

of the latest news. Although Layla could speak and understand English, she could not read or write it.

Mikael was in the news a lot at the moment, defending a man accused of murder and other heinous crimes against his late partner. Layla had been closely following the case from her computer after she went to bed at night.

How she loved the news clips of Mikael walking out of court in his black robe and wig. He offered no comment or apology to the questions that were hurled at him. He seemed not to care that everyone was demanding to know how he could even consider defending such a vile man.

Perhaps Mikael would be glad to turn his focus to a family matter, Layla thought. Maybe he would welcome the break from his horrible client, because Mikael did not look happy.

Not once had she seen him smile.

Layla felt a small shiver as she enlarged an image and looked at his full mouth. It was the only soft feature in his face, and it had her tongue rolling over her lips. His hair was as dark as his skin was pale, and always his attire was immaculate. Oh, and his voice—*his voice*!

She clicked on a rare interview from a couple of years ago that she had recently found. It was Layla's very favourite one, and she listened to his deep, heavily accented voice scolding a reporter.

'Tread carefully!' He pointed his finger at the reporter though for Layla it was if he was scolding her and Layla made a biting noise with her teeth. Her smile was wide as she started at the screen. 'May I remind you of the unanimous verdict?'

She had not chosen Mikael for his beauty, and yet the more she looked at him, and the more she found out about him, the more Layla wanted to know. She looked into his serious grey eyes—cold eyes that made her feel warm.

Some of the pictures of Mikael Layla was not so keen on—for there were a few of him with very beautiful women by his side.

Many beautiful women.

There he was on a yacht, with a blonde beauty lying topless on a daybed—or Layla assumed she was topless, because where her nipples should be the picture was all blurry.

Layla found her lips were pursed, but then she shrugged.

Her brother Zahid had been wild in his day.

She did not want wild—she wanted fun and romance and dancing.

Of course she would return to Ishla intact.

There were simply some things that Layla wanted to experience before she married a man she did not love. She closed the computer and lay on her back, imagining a whole day spent in bed without having to dress or speak to another person. She thought of other things too, like a romantic dinner, sitting holding hands, and afterwards dancing—which was forbidden in Ishla. She imagined the brush of lips on her mouth… But then her eyes snapped open, for it was Mikael's mouth that she was imagining.

No.

Layla dismissed that thought.

Mikael was merely a means to an end.

And a commoner too!

She clicked on her laptop again, to see if any other foreign royals were visiting Australia, and sighed at the lack of news for there were a couple of foreign princes who looked as if they could be fun!

Jamila, Layla's handmaiden, knocked on the door, and Layla clicked onto a game of chess she was playing and then called for Jamila to come in and prepare her bath.

When it was ready Layla went through and stood by the sunken bath as Jamila undressed her and then held Layla's hand as she lowered herself in.

'The water is lovely,' she said as Jamila started to wash her. 'Jamila?' Layla's voice was just a little too high as she attempted to sound casual. 'Are you nervous about coming to Australia?' When Jamila didn't answer straight away, Layla jumped in. 'Because if you are I can speak with father. I am sure I would manage on my own.'

'I would be more nervous if you were in a foreign country without me to take care of you,' Jamila said.

Jamila adored Layla. She had held her the moment she was born—a few moments before Layla's mother had died.

Layla was the baby Jamila had never had—not that she could ever let Layla know that she loved her like a daughter.

Neither could Jamila tell a single soul that she secretly loved Fahid—the King—and no one must ever know about the occasional love they shared.

'Here.' Jamila handed Layla a cloth, which she took, and she washed her private parts as Jamila washed her hair.

Still Layla carried on speaking.

'Well, you should rest while we are in Australia,' Layla said. 'You deserve to have a holiday too.'

'Layla!' Jamila's shrewd eyes narrowed as she rubbed oil into Layla's long black mane of hair. 'What are you up to?'

'Nothing.' Layla shrugged her bony shoulders. 'I just think that it would be nice for you to have a chance to rest and relax.'

Layla said no more, but she *was* worried about

how her plans might affect Jamila, who was old and very set in her ways.

Trinity and Zahid, Layla had decided, would just have to bear the chaos of her actions. After all, they had had their fun—but poor Jamila...

Layla swallowed and dismissed the gnaw of discontent. She certainly wasn't going to change her plans to spare a servant's feelings.

'You are too thin,' Jamila said as she looked at Layla's skinny knees jutting up out of the water, her slender arms wrapped around them.

'Jamila,' Layla said, 'I could fill this bath and you would still say that I was too thin. Do you remember when I was a baby and always hungry and you said that I was too fat?'

Jamila's hand paused as she went to rinse Layla's hair—Layla should not remember those times. Jamila thought of those little fat legs and arms and her round belly. Layla had been such an angry, demanding baby and toddler. She had begged for attention from her father and it had been denied her as he'd grieved deeply for Annan, the late Queen. Jamila had tried to comfort the little princess with food, feeding her cream, honey, anything that might stop the relentless sobs that filled the palace.

Such sad, sad times.

'Let us get you dressed,' Jamila said, quickly finishing Layla's hair. 'Your father wishes to speak with you before you leave.'

Layla had chosen a simple burnt orange cotton tunic for the journey, but Jamila prepared a silver robe and silver jewelled slippers for her to wear on her arrival as there would be some dignitaries to greet them. Her fingers, toes and ears were dressed in pretty jewels, and her long black hair was tied in a low bun which was worn at the side of her head.

'Dismissed,' Layla said to Jamila, and then frowned when still she stood there.

'You *will* listen to what your father has to say, won't you?' Jamila asked, for she too was worried at the thought of Layla beyond the palace walls.

'Dismissed, Jamila,' Layla said.

Alone, Layla stepped out onto the balcony. The sun was starting to set and the sky was a fiery orange. The desert was like molten gold and it was a sight to behold, a view that she loved, and yet she knew there was more. She looked up to the sky, through which she would soon be being carried to her long-awaited adventure.

She knew she was being bad, and yet she had tried so hard to be good.

Once this was over she would be good for ever, Layla vowed.

This was her last chance.

Four years ago, when she was twenty, Layla had been dressed in white and gold and led down the stairs to walk into a room and select her husband from the men who knelt there.

Hussain had been and still was considered the right choice. They had played as children, and her father had told her that marrying Hussain would bring many benefits to the people of Ishla. Yet as Layla had walked down the stairs she had remembered what a mean little boy Hussain had been, and she had collapsed and started to shout and scream.

The kind palace doctor had smoothed out the

offence caused by explaining that anxiety had caused the young princess to have a seizure.

Layla smiled to the sky. She had not selected her husband that day.

It had not been a seizure, just her temper exploding as she had looked at her wrist and recalled one time with Hussain.

'How do you make a match burn twice?' he had asked when Layla was nine.

'Show me?'

Wide-eyed, Layla had watched as he had lit the match and blown it out and then dug the burning sulphur into her wrist.

Immediately Layla had slapped him.

Now she looked down to the small scar on her otherwise unblemished skin and wondered about Hussain's reaction if his wife were to slap him.

He had no doubt moved on from matches now!

Layla headed back inside and opened the drawer in her dresser. Feeling far into the back, she removed the wrapped parcel she had been hiding.

Opening it, she held in her palm the black ruby named Opium. It had been gifted to her at birth by the King of Bishram and must surely be worth quite a lot.

Layla hoped that it was.

She had read that Mikael was expensive, and perhaps he would want to be paid.

Layla slipped the ruby into her tunic, worrying about something she had read on the internet about Australian Customs. She tried to tell herself that it would all be okay.

She made her way through the palace to her father's study, where Abdul, the King's chief aide, let her in. But Fahid dismissed Abdul so that he could speak to his daughter alone.

'Are you looking forward to your trip?' Fahid asked her.

'Very much, Father.'

'When you are in the hotel you will have your own room, with Jamila adjoining. Jamila is to take care of you there, but at all other times you are to be with either Trinity or Zahid.'

'I know that.'

'If you are in a restaurant then Trinity is to come with you if you need to go to—'

'Father!' Layla interrupted. 'I *do* know the rules.'

'They are there for your protection,' the King said. He looked at his daughter, whom he loved so very much. She was so contrary—floaty and vague, and yet arrogant too, just as her mother Annan had been. Layla was fiercely independent, and yet naïve from living her life within the palace grounds.

'Layla, I have not asked to speak with you to deliver meaningless words and a lecture. I really want you to listen to all that I have to say. Things are very different overseas—the people are different too. There is traffic...' The King winced as he thought of his daughter in a foreign city with fast-moving cars when she had never so much as crossed a road.

Layla saw his grimace and her heart went out to her father. 'I know you are worried for me, Father,' she said. 'I know that you have loved me from the moment that I was born...'

Again the King closed his eyes as Layla hit a still raw nerve.

He *hadn't* loved her from the moment she was born.

In fact the King had rejected Layla for more than a year. Sometimes Fahid wondered if that was why Layla was so rebellious and constantly challenged him, even if she couldn't logically know about that time.

He worried so much about her—especially knowing that soon he would be gone from his world. Surely Layla needed a stern husband like Hussain, who would keep her in line?

He would just miss the wild Layla so...

'Do you have any questions you wish to ask?' Fahid offered.

'I do.' Layla nodded. 'Father, I was looking up the customs in Australia—I thought I would find out who curtsies to me, who bows, and what gifts we should exchange, but instead I read that at the airport your property can be searched—even your body...' She paused when she saw her father's re-action. 'Why are you laughing?'

'Oh, Layla!' The King wiped his eyes as he tried to halt his laughter. 'That does not apply to *you.*

Your retinue will take care of all the paperwork and luggage and our gifts are in the diplomatic pouch. You do not have to concern yourself with such things.'

'Thank you, Father.'

He rose from his seat and came over and took her in his arms. 'I love you, Layla.'

'I love you too,' Layla said, and hugged him back, but there were tears filling her eyes as she did so. 'I am sorry if I make you cross at times—please know that it doesn't mean I don't love you.'

'I know that,' Fahid said.

What the King didn't know, though, was that Layla was not apologising for her past.

Instead she was saying sorry for all that was to come.

CHAPTER TWO

'GREAT!'

Mikael had no choice but to pull to a stop as a policeman put up his hand and halted the morning traffic.

Even though he had more than enough on his mind, with closing arguments starting this morning, he flicked on the news to listen to the traffic report and hopefully find out the reason for the hold-up. He knew that he should have stayed at his city apartment, or even a hotel, instead of driving to his waterfront home last night, but he had just needed to get away from the case.

Mikael's remote beachside home was his haven, and last night he had needed to escape from the more pungent details of the case he was consumed by and breathe in fresh air and simply switch off.

It would be over soon, Mikael told himself.

'*Pizdet.*' He cursed in Russian when he found out that the reason for the delay was some visiting royal family, grinding everyone else to a halt.

Then he heard a little about himself as the news continued.

Mikael Romanov, SC, was surely going to lose this time…there was no way he could get his client off…

Then the calls in from listeners started and a character assassination ensued. Not of his client but himself.

'What sort of a person *is* Romanov?' an enraged caller asked. 'How can he possibly sleep at night?'

Mikael yawned with boredom and turned the radio off.

When his phone rang, instead of letting it go to voicemail, as he usually would, Mikael saw that it was Demyan and took the call.

'Any news?' Mikael asked, because Demyan's wife Alina was due to give birth soon.

'We have a little girl—Annika.' Demyan said, and Mikael rolled his eyes at the sound of his tough friend sounding so emotional. 'She's beautiful. Her hair is curly, like Alina's...'

Demyan went on to describe interminable details to Mikael.

All babies had blue eyes, Mikael thought.

'Congratulations,' Mikael said. 'Am I to visit while Alina is still in the hospital? What is the protocol?'

Demyan laughed. He took no offence. He knew that Mikael had no concept of family, for Mikael's upbringing had been even harsher than Demyan's.

'You don't have to come to the hospital,' Demyan said, 'but once this case is over it would be good if you could visit us before you disappear onto your yacht. I'm really looking forward to showing Annika off.'

'I'll be there,' Mikael said. 'It is closing arguments over the next couple of days, and then we await the verdict.'

'How is the trial going?' Demyan asked. 'It is all over the news.'

'Long,' came Mikael's honest answer. 'It has been a very long couple of months.'

It had been an isolated couple of months too.

He always pretty much locked himself away from the world during a trial and, he admitted to Demyan, he was more than a little jaded from sitting with his client day in, day out.

'He's a fortunate man to have such a good solicitor.'

'Barrister,' Mikael corrected. 'One day you will get it right. Anyway, enough about the trial. Go back to your beautiful wife and daughter, I am very pleased to hear the good news.'

Rather you than me, Mikael thought as he ended the call.

When Demyan had told him that he was marrying again Mikael had offered to draw up a watertight pre-nup this time, given how Demyan's first wife had ripped him off for years.

Demyan had refused.

Fool! Mikael had not just thought it but had said it straight to Demyan's face, but he had been told that he was far too cynical.

Guilty!

Absolutely Mikael was cynical—he believed

nothing anyone told him and had been proved right numerous times.

Mikael trusted and needed no one in his life, for he had never *had* anyone.

There were a few vague memories of a communal flat when he was growing up, but not one person in particular he'd been able to turn to. Mikael had been his own protector—even when he had found himself on the streets.

Especially then.

When he was a teenager Igor, a government worker, had stepped in and given Mikael an identity, a surname, an assumed date of birth and then a home.

Igor was the reason Mikael was driving to chambers now to prepare for court—*he* was the reason Mikael believed absolutely in the need for a solid defence. For without one justice could never be truly served.

He did not want to think today of Igor; instead his eyes moved from the procession of royal cars to his dashboard, where the mileage read six hundred and forty-nine. He would be bored with his new toy by the time it read one thousand, but for now the low silver sports car was *his* new baby.

Finally the procession passed and the traffic inched forward.

Mikael arrived at chambers and spoke to Wendy, his clerk, for a few moments. His world had centred around this trial for a very long while, and all he wanted was the arguments delivered, the jury out, the verdict in and then to get away.

He'd take one of his toys to the water—he didn't even want crew.

Then Mikael changed his mind.

A couple of crew might be essential.

He had no intention of cooking or cleaning.

Perhaps Mandy could join him for a couple of days too?

Or Pearl?

Mikael soon put all such thoughts out of his mind and sat for a quiet period in his office, preparing himself for the day ahead and getting back to the real love of his life.

The letter of the law.

CHAPTER THREE

'I WANT TO drive that car!' Layla's slender finger pointed to a low silver sports car that gleamed in the morning sun as they passed an intersection.

'You can't drive,' Zahid said, but he did smile—it was nice to see Layla so excited and animated. Her face was up against the blacked-out window as she watched the world go by unseen, fascinated by it all.

'When can it just be us?' she asked. 'I am tired of all the formalities.'

'Soon,' Zahid said. 'Once we are at the hotel things will be more relaxed.'

'We can go shopping then,' Trinity added.

'Just Trinity and I?' Layla checked with her brother who, after a brief hesitation, nodded.

'Good.' Layla smiled. 'I want a red dress, red shoes, red...'

Her list went on until they were at the hotel.

Soon the Ishla royals and their retinue were taking up the entire top floor. There were guards at the lift and Layla paced her suite nervously, waiting for Trinity to come and take her shopping.

'Let me do your hair again,' Jamila offered.

'My hair is fine,' Layla said. 'You can go and rest in your room now.'

'I will wait for Trinity to get here.'

'You are dismissed, Jamila.' Layla said.

All Layla wanted was to be alone with her thoughts and to go over her plans for a minute or two before Trinity arrived.

Reluctantly Jamila went to her adjoining room. Layla looked at the lock on the door that stood between them and wanted to turn it.

She wouldn't have to turn it, Layla reminded herself.

A few hours from now she would be free!

Layla looked down at the streets below. Soon she would be down there amongst the noise and people.

She could see yellow taxis everywhere.

It was going to work!

'Enter,' Layla said when there was a knock at the door.

'Layla, you have to open it from the inside!' Trinity called.

'Oh!'

Fancy that.

Layla was ready to go, but Trinity seemed to have other ideas.

Zahid's last words to Trinity had been, 'Watch her.' She looked at Layla, dressed in a long silver tunic and jewelled slippers. Her black hair had been taken out of the bun and was loose and glossy. Her absolute beauty would turn heads everywhere they went.

'Would you like...?' Trinity hesitated—she was still very new to being Zahid's wife, and sometimes she simply didn't know how to speak to Layla, who was so different from Trinity's serious, rather more grounded husband. 'Would you like to borrow some of my clothes to wear while we go shopping?' Trinity offered.

'Borrow?' Layla screwed up her nose.

'I'm just concerned that in what you're wearing you'll stand out and people might stare.'

'But I always stand out,' Layla said, 'and people always stare. Come on—let us go shopping. I have been looking forward to this for a long time.'

They passed the guards and took the elevator down, and then stepped out onto the hot, busy street. Layla was more than used to heat, and walked quickly ahead.

'Slow down,' Trinity said. 'There's no rush.'

They wandered into boutique after boutique, but Layla was not really looking at the clothes—instead she was wondering how she could shrug Trinity off, for she was watching Layla like a hawk would watch its prey.

'I would like to try that,' Layla said, pointing to an ice cream shop.

'Sounds good.'

Still Trinity clung to her, and Layla's impatience was increasing. Yes, the ice cream was refreshing, but would Trinity ever just give her five minutes to be alone?

'Where to now?' Trinity asked once they had finished their ice creams.

'I might go for a little wander,' Layla said casually.

'Layla...' Trinity swallowed. 'Zahid said that I wasn't to leave you alone.'

'I am not a baby,' Layla said, 'I am twenty-four...'

But she went to cross the road without so much as looking and Trinity grabbed her back just in time.

'You have to wait for the lights to change before you cross.' Trinity pointed to the traffic lights as they turned green and they started to cross. 'I'm not leaving you alone, Layla. You can take it up with Zahid this evening if you want to, but for now...'

Trinity's voice trailed off as they walked across the road and Layla looked to where Trinity's eyes had been drawn.

Perfect!

'Oh, look,' Layla said, walking over to the window of the baby boutique that held Trinity in its spell. 'Oh, Trinity, look at these sweet clothes—

there is nothing like this in Ishla…' From Trinity's rapt expression, Layla knew her chance to escape was surely about to come. 'Let's go in.'

They did just that.

It wasn't just clothes on display but teeny-tiny shoes and socks, and little cashmere baby blankets too, and of *course*, the assistant told Trinity, they'd be only too happy to ship to Ishla.

'Why would you use a ship when we have a plane?' Layla asked, but Trinity wasn't listening—instead she was gazing at those little blankets and had the lost look in her eyes that Layla recognised from her cousins who had had babies.

Layla slipped outside unnoticed, pulling an envelope out of her bag as she did so. If Trinity saw her Layla would say she was just stepping out for some air.

On the street there was a yellow cab driving towards her, and Layla put up her hand as the clips she had watched on her computer had shown her she should.

It obeyed!

The driver did not get out and open the door for

her, which made Layla cross, and she was glad that the window was wound down as the driver asked her where she wanted to go for it was a very smelly car.

Layla gave him Mikael's address. 'I need you to hurry.'

She *did* need him to hurry, for Trinity was racing out of the boutique.

'Layla, wait!' she shouted.

'I shall be fine, Trinity.' Layla threw the letter she had written in Arabic out of the window and shouted instructions to Trinity as the taxi pulled away. 'Get Zahid to read this and do *not* tell my father.'

She refused to feel guilty for ruining their honeymoon. Okay, maybe she felt a *little* guilty—but, Layla reminded herself, Zahid had had this sort of freedom for close to two decades when he had lived in England. Trinity had had it all her life.

Layla just wanted a week.

Mikael's day had not improved—not that he let anyone know it. He sat with his face impassive as he listened to the closing arguments from the prosecution barrister, who boo-hooed where Mikael had been expecting him to. A couple of members of the jury were even in tears. But then the prosecution hit him with an argument Mikael had not foreseen.

Deliberately Mikael refused to reach for his notes or react.

He just noted it in his head.

Tomorrow his response would be savage.

Tomorrow he would use every letter of the law that he had at his disposal.

'I'm gone, aren't I?' his client said before heading back to the cells.

'I haven't closed yet,' Mikael responded, though he gave no pep talk. He certainly wasn't here to reassure or make friends with his clients. All he required from himself was to offer the best defence.

It was a long walk back to chambers.

The press were waiting, with their usual questions, and Mikael duly ignored them. His mouth was dry and he wanted the cool darkness of his office, where the heavy drapes would be closed and he could sit in silence and make notes on all that had been said today.

'Don't ask!' Mikael warned his clerk as he stepped in.

Both knew that it was not going well, and that he would be here all night working on the final details before delivering his closing speech to-morrow.

'I don't know how to tell you this—' Wendy started.

Mikael turned and saw that his very efficient clerk for once looked a touch ruffled.

'There's a lady here to see you.'

'I haven't got time to see anyone now.'

'Mikael, I've tried to get rid of her...' Wendy let out a nervous laugh. 'I've never met anyone like her before—you simply can't say no. I even ended up paying for her taxi because she didn't have any money—the driver was about to call the police!'

'Wendy?' Mikael frowned, because he had never seen his clerk like this. Mikael dealt with the lowest of the low, and had only the best of staff around him—staff that were able to deal with the most difficult of people. 'Where is she?' he asked, glancing into the small waiting room.

'She's waiting in your office.'

'What?' She'd got past Wendy? This Mikael had to see. 'What's her name?'

'She won't tell me,' Wendy said, 'and she won't tell me what she's here for either. She refuses to discuss it with anyone but you.'

'Okay.' Mikael nodded. 'Don't worry. I shall sort it out.'

Mikael walked into his office and completely ignored his uninvited guest, who was standing by the window, looking out through a chink in the heavy curtains and watching the world go by.

Yet as much as he ignored her somehow Mikael was reminded of the rare beauty of the first glimpse of a new moon. Perhaps it was the way the light caught her silver robe or because she was so slender, but as he opened the bar fridge it was that image that was on his mind.

'Mr Romanov!'

Her voice demanded that he acknowledge her.

'Oh, sorry...' Mikael's voice was wry as, his back to her, he added a slice of lime and ice to a glass and then poured sparkling water. 'Weren't you getting enough attention?'

'I expect to be greeted.'

'Well, had you made an appointment then you would have been.'

He turned and looked at her, a golden ray of sun from the chink in the curtains serving as his spotlight. Her beauty was now possibly the biggest challenge of his day, for Mikael was momentarily sideswiped. Her black eyes were huge in her exquisite face, her hair thick and glossy, and her complexion quite simply flawless. His eyes roamed her face—as far as Mikael could tell she wasn't even wearing make-up. She was the first woman to actually stun him—so much so that when she held out her hand Mikael handed her his drink.

How did that happen? Mikael wondered as he turned again and made another drink—for himself this time.

'I am Princess Layla of Ishla,' Layla said, because, given Mikael's poor manners, perhaps he was not aware of to whom he was speaking.

'Really?' Mikael said.

Layla waited for him to continue.

'So *you're* the reason I was almost late for court this morning.'

'Excuse me?'

'Your convoy held me up,' Mikael said. 'Look, I don't know what your issue is—in fact I don't even *want* to know. I'm in the middle of a very complicated case and I am going on leave soon.'

'I know all about your case, but I need for you to speak with my brother. I want you tell him that I am taking a week off from royal duty and that he is not to look for me or inform my father.'

'Can't *you* tell him that?'

'I have written it all in a letter that he must be reading about now. I need you to reiterate the contents to him,' Layla said. 'If I speak with him it will get all emotional and I might back down— that is why I want you to do it for me.'

'You need an embassy.'

'No,' Layla shook her head. 'I do not want to make a big incident—unless I *have* to, of course.'

He heard the warning note in her voice, saw then the fire in her eyes, and he understood why Wendy had been unable to say no to her. She was pretty unstoppable.

Mikael, though, could not be manipulated. 'As I just said, I am near the end of a huge case. I'm not taking anything else on.'

'You will make one phone call for me,' Layla said. 'But first you can arrange for some refreshments to be brought in.' It had been a long afternoon of shopping after all.

Mikael felt the shock from the muscles in his face as they broke into a smile.

Was she for real?

'You want me to arrange refreshments *before* I make your phone call?'

'Just something light.' Layla nodded. 'Maybe some fruit, and also something sweet.'

Mikael pulled out a roll of mints. 'Here's your refreshments.'

She took one and popped it in her mouth, and

he watched her eyes widen in delight as she rolled the mint across her tongue.

'I like.'

So too, Mikael decided, did he!

CHAPTER FOUR

'ONE PHONE CALL,' Mikael said.

But there was no way, Mikael knew, that this was going to go away with one phone call. He had only agreed to it because Layla had eked from him the first smile he had given in weeks.

He opened the curtains and invited her to take a seat.

'First, though—' Mikael went on, but Layla interrupted.

'I give you some details.'

'No,' Mikael said. 'First we need to discuss my retainer.'

'Retainer?'

'I'm very expensive,' Mikael said.

'Oh, you want payment up-front?'

'Absolutely.'

'I have this.'

Mikael was a master at keeping his face impassive—poker would have been a lucrative hobby if he'd so chosen—but even he was struggling as, from her tunic, Layla took out a stone that looked more like a paperweight and placed it on the desk between them.

'It is called Opium,' Layla explained. 'It is a rare black ruby that was gifted to me by the King of Bishram on my birth, so I would expect it to be worth quite a bit.'

Mikael said nothing at first. He just stared at the stone that was almost as beautiful as its owner and thought of her walking the streets with that in her pocket. After a long stretch of silence he picked it up and decided to put it in his safe for now, then he sat back at his desk and looked at her. 'What exactly are you hoping to achieve this week?'

'There are things that I would like to do before I marry.'

'Such as?'

'They are not your concern. All I want is a week of freedom from my duties and a week away from my family.'

'To do what?' Mikael persisted. 'If I'm to ring your brother then I need to know what you intend to get up to.'

'I would like to dance,' Layla said. 'It is forbidden in Ishla. And I would like to try an Irish coffee....'

'There *are* other drinks.' Mikael smirked.

'My brother mentioned Irish coffee once, many years ago. I thought it sounded nice that the cream stays at the top.'

'What else?'

Layla looked across the table at Mikael. For the first time in her life she felt a little... Layla tried to decide *how* she felt. Intimidated? She wasn't sure if that was the right word, but it had never entered her head that Mikael might say no to her request. More than that, though, the effect of his smile had unsettled her stomach in a way she did not understand.

Certainly she wasn't about to tell him all the adventures she was seeking—though her eyes did fall to his mouth, which she had briefly imagined upon hers, but then she met again the cool of his gaze. 'I don't know you well enough to tell you,' Layla said.

'How long have you been planning this?'

'For quite some time,' Layla admitted.

'Would your family have guessed that you were going to escape?'

'No.' Immediately she shook her head.

''You're sure of that.'

'Very sure,' she said. 'I learnt a very long time ago that I get in trouble if I tell anyone my thoughts.'

'You can be honest here,' Mikael said, and Layla gave a hesitant nod—though her eyes said that she doubted it.

She did offer a little more. 'I tried to get my brother to take me to a wedding in London a few months ago—I was going to escape there, but he refused to take me with him.'

Sensible man, Mikael thought, feeling a knot of unease forming at the thought of her let loose in London—or even let loose here, for there was an innocence behind her arrogance, an inherent trust in the good of others that could so easily be shattered.

'How are your family going to react?'

'That depends,' Layla responded. 'I have made it very clear in my letter to my brother that he is not to inform my father that I am missing. If he does my father will have no choice but to create an international incident. That is avoidable, of course—I just need for you to reassure my brother that I will be safe and that I will return to the hotel one week from now.'

'What about your mother?'

'From what I have been told about her, she would approve.'

'Told?'

'She is dead, but apparently we are very similar, and if that is the case then she'd approve of my plans.'

'Where are you going to stay?' Mikael asked. 'Have you got friends…?'

'You will arrange that.'

'*One* phone call?' Mikael reminded her.

'Two.' Layla smiled. 'You are to make sure I

stay somewhere nice and you will have to drive me there. I am not taking a taxi again; the man was very rude.'

'Possibly because you didn't pay him,' Mikael said. 'I'll ask Wendy to book you somewhere and she'll drive you to a hotel.'

They went over a few more details. There was nothing uncomplicated about Layla. She was twenty-four, he found out, and he checked that she was healthy, that she wasn't on any medication, or suffering any illnesses. He wanted to be sure that there was nothing that could be flashed up on the news about her life being at risk.

Physically, it would seem she was healthy—though certifiable, perhaps...

'They thought that I had seizure once, but I did not,' Layla said.

Mikael let out a tense breath as out of her lips popped another surprise.

'I was on my way to select a husband and I started to scream and shout expletives and then I fell to the floor. The palace doctor is kind and she told my father and suitors that anxiety had caused a seizure. But it was not a seizure. I was just cross.'

'Don't you ever try that trick on me,' Mikael warned her.

'It wasn't a trick.'

'Oh, Layla.' Mikael slowly shook his head. 'I'm quite sure that you are full of them.' He ran shrewd eyes over the cunning minx. 'Why did you choose me?'

'Because you are not swayed by emotion and you don't care what others think.'

'You don't know that,' Mikael said.

'You are hated by many for the people you defend.' Layla shrugged. 'Yet you do not look like a man who cries himself to sleep at night. Now, am I wasting my time or are you going to make that call?'

'Layla…'

'*Princess* Layla,' she corrected.

'I'd suggest,' Mikael responded, 'that if you really want to disappear for a week then you lose the title.'

'Mr Romanov—'

'Mikael,' he interrupted.

'Mikael,' Layla amended. 'I would like you to speak with my brother now.'

'Very well,' Mikael said, 'but you need to understand that I am near the end of a very complex case. I will make one phone call and have you taken to a hotel...' He briefly closed his eyes. 'I don't have time to babysit you.'

'Good.'

She smiled very widely then, and it was like a fist to Mikael's guts because the breath was almost knocked out of him when she did.

'The last thing I want this week is to be watched over.'

Layla didn't have a phone, but she did have Zahid's number. Mikael blocked his own number and then made the call.

He did not give his name, but explained that he was representing Layla and that her request for a week away from her family was far from unreasonable.

'You don't understand—' Zahid started.

'I understand that the laws in your land may be different,' Mikael interrupted, 'but—'

'You don't understand *Layla*.' This time it was Zahid who broke in.

Far from the fury and hysterics that Mikael had expected, Zahid's response was clipped. 'She will not manage alone.'

'Layla is twenty-four.'

'Which means for twenty-four years she has had everything done for her. *Everything*,' Zahid reiterated.

'Well, she seems very capable to me, and more than independent.'

'Could I speak with her?' Zahid asked.

Mikael looked over to Layla, who sat rigid in the chair, her lips pursed. 'Your brother wishes to speak with you.'

He expected her to shake her head, but instead Layla nodded.

'You don't have to,' he said, but she was holding her hand out for the phone.

'Don't give him my name,' Mikael warned her.

Layla had been right to get him in to handle

this, Mikael thought, because whatever was being said in Arabic the conversation was clearly emotional. He watched as she stood and started pacing, shouting and crying, but then, just as he was going to take the phone from her, she switched to English.

'No, Trinity, I do not accept what Zahid just said and you can tell him the same. Yes, I have messed up your honeymoon—well, guess what? I don't expect to *have* a happy honeymoon. I *know* my honeymoon will be miserable. At least you get the rest of your life to be happy…'

Mikael's eyes widened a touch in admiration, and then he suppressed the second smile to grace his lips in months as Layla continued.

'What does your pregnancy have to do with *my* life?' Layla demanded. 'I am supposed to put my *one* chance for freedom to the side because you are growing a baby…?' Layla gave an incredulous laugh. 'I never realised you were so precious, Trinity. Let me speak with my brother—clearly you are supposed to avoid the real world for the next six months.'

Mikael listened as she continued speaking to Trinity, who was surely pleading with her to go back before the situation got out of hand.

'I think one week of freedom is a very good deal,' Layla said. 'And I warn you: if you tell my father—if you look for me—then I shall take my barrister's advice and go to an embassy.' Layla handed Mikael the phone. 'My brother wants to speak with you again.'

'Whoever you are—' Zahid's voice was still supremely calm but it cracked near the end of his words '—please look after her.'

Mikael was just about to point out that that wasn't in his job description, but then he looked over to Layla.

How could he send her out onto the streets alone?

'She'll be fine,' Mikael said.

'I need your word.'

'Hey,' Mikael said, 'you're not my client.'

'I'll be paying your bill,' Zahid said, and Mikael

ended the call and threw the phone on the desk and looked at his problem.

'You are trouble,' he said, and Layla smiled.

'I know that I am.'

CHAPTER FIVE

WHERE TO HOUSE the runaway princess? Mikael thought as her eyes lit on his chessboard and she walked across his office.

'Leave it!' he warned, because he played against himself and chess was part of his process when he was working through a case and needed fifteen minutes away from it at a time.

'But I can see checkmate!' Layla said.

'Layla!' Mikael warned again, and strode over. 'Leave it!'

He pointed his finger at her and blinked as her teeth made a biting noise and she smiled widely at him.

She was like a little wild animal.

Sex had previously been the last thing on his mind.

That would happen after the trial—*as soon as*

possible after the trial—when Mikael would make up for all he had missed out on as he surfaced to the world.

Sex, though, was right at the front of his mind now—and starting to make itself known elsewhere.

'Come on.' His voice was brusque as he opened his office door. 'Wendy…' he called as Layla followed him out, but then Mikael halted. It would be easier to drop her off himself than explain it all to Wendy, so they walked together to his car.

'This is *your* car!' Layla clearly approved. 'It is very beautiful.'

'Thank you.'

'I'd love to drive it.'

'But then I'd have to kill you,' Mikael said, opening the passenger side door for her.

'You are much more polite than the taxi driver,' Layla said.

Mikael got in himself and before driving off called his favourite hotel.

He glanced over to Layla. Yes, he told Reservations, he would have his usual luxury suite.

'Right, I've booked you into a hotel. I'll cover it, and we can sort out money some other time.'

'You have your retainer.'

'I do.' Mikael sighed, imagining trying to cash a rare ruby. 'Put your seatbelt on.'

'Pardon?' Layla frowned. 'The taxi driver said the same.'

'And did you?'

Clearly not.

'You need to.'

It should have been easy to reach over and do it himself, except she started to laugh as if he was tickling her as he leant over to retrieve the belt and suddenly there was nothing straightforward about the way Mikael was feeling as his nostrils delivered to his brain its first hit of the exotic aroma of Layla close up.

'What *are* you doing?' She was giddy from the brief contact.

'Putting on your seatbelt.' He pulled the belt out, trying to ignore the scent of her and the sound of her laughter as he clicked it in. 'Don't you wear seatbelts in Ishla?'

'*I* don't,' Layla said. 'The same thing happened on the plane.' Then she turned and looked at him. 'Though it wasn't as much fun.'

Mikael said nothing. He just drove to the hotel. But he could feel her eyes on him.

'You're not a very happy person, are you?' Layla observed.

'It's not a requisite for my job.'

'You're not working now.'

'Yes, Layla,' Mikael said, 'I am. Believe me, it would have been far cheaper to get a chauffeur-driven limousine with a trained monkey in the back peeling grapes for you than to have me drive you.' He turned and saw her frown. 'You'll see the breakdown on my bill.'

'I want that monkey!' Layla said, then pouted when she got no response from Mikael. 'You didn't laugh at my joke.'

'I wasn't sure if it *was* one,' he admitted, but then turned and gave her a brief smile. 'It was a good one, though!'

They got out at the hotel and Mikael gave the parking attendant his keys, telling him he'd be out shortly and not to park the car. They walked through to check in.

'I'll see you to your room and then I need to go back and do some work.'

'That's fine.'

Heads were turning, Mikael realised, and not just turning. People were craning their necks to get a glimpse of Layla as she glided along beside him. As he checked her in under his name he explained that there was no luggage.

'You might want to…' He turned to see if she needed some cash but she was no longer beside him. Mikael saw her wandering into one of the hotel's boutiques.

'Excuse me a moment,' he said to the receptionist, and then strode through the foyer and into the boutique.

'I like!' Layla said, holding up a very glittery, very high shoe. She sat down and kicked off her silver slipper and held out her foot to him, just as the assistant called over that she would be there in a moment.

Even her feet were beautiful, Mikael thought.

Long and slender and, yes, clearly irresistible—because with barely a thought he was helping her on with the shoe.

The sole of her foot was a soft as a kitten's paw and Mikael tried to ignore the feel of her skin and the scent of her hair as she bent forward as he tried to slip it on.

'It doesn't fit!' Layla exclaimed.

'You're like Cinderella in reverse.'

'Why doesn't it fit?' Layla demanded, because in Ishla her shoes were hand-made and fitted beautifully. *This* she could not even get her foot in.

'Because this isn't Planet Layla,' Mikael said. 'Come on.'

'But I want—'

'Layla.' His voice was stern. Mikael was fast losing patience as she followed him to the elevators. 'I don't have time to be taking you shoe-shopping, I deliver my closing argument tomorrow...'

Not that she'd understand that, Mikael thought as he swiped a card for the lift and handed it to her. 'You need to use this to take the lift and to get into your suite.'

'Thank you.'

'Twenty-fourth floor,' Mikael said, pressing the button.

'How did court go today?' Layla asked.

'Not very well.'

'He must be very difficult to defend,' Layla said.

Mikael shrugged and offered his usual response to that statement. 'Not difficult for me,' he said.

'It's an interesting case, though,' Layla said. 'Her silence is his defence.'

He had assumed that she was talking morally.

For once he was wrong.

'You really *have* been following it.' Mikael didn't even hide the slight surprise in his voice.

'Of course,' Layla said. 'I wanted to know who I would be dealing with.'

He showed her around the suite and where everything was, and then he showed her the phone. 'If you want anything ring—'

'You.'

'No, you ring the desk.'

'What if I need to speak with you?'

'Please don't need to speak with me,' he said.

He went to get out his business card but then changed his mind and wrote his personal number down on a pad on the desk.

'Emergencies only,' he warned, but she wasn't listening. She was at the window, her eyes glittering as she eyed the city streets below. He was starting to understand Zahid's concern—because how the hell would she manage out there?

'Can I ask that you don't go out tonight?'

She briefly turned and gave him a scoffing look. 'You think I did all this just to stay in my room?'

'Layla, I have a huge case on.' Mikael let out a breath. 'But tomorrow night I'll take you out.'

'Really?'

'Or possibly the next night.'

Layla rolled her eyes. 'Good evening, Mikael, thank you for your help with my brother. You're dismissed for today.'

He could not dismiss her from his mind, though.

Well, he'd have to.

Mikael returned to chambers and finally sat down to work through his closing argument. If he was lucky he'd get a couple of hours' sleep.

Mikael was very good at shutting the world out when needed.

This was his passion.

Over and over the prosecution's closing he went, looking for holes, for the one little thing that might plant reasonable doubt.

He already had it—in fact Mikael had long known that it was *all* he had. Layla had got it exactly: the victim's silence was his client's only defence.

He might be getting more than two hours' sleep after all, he thought, and his mind briefly drifted to Layla. He wondered how she was doing in a strange city on her first night out of Ishla.

Not his problem.

He walked over to the chessboard to take a small break and stared at it for ages.

It wasn't even close to checkmate.

Was it?

Mikael looked again, for a considerably longer time.

No.

He made his move.

Mikael got back to his computer screen but there was a gnawing of anxiety in his mind. To ease it he picked up the phone and called the hotel and asked what had been charged to his room.

Several Irish coffees, toiletries and two peeled and thinly sliced apples, he was told for starters. But then that gnaw started to burn as he heard about the dresses and shoes that had also been charged to the suite, and that the car was almost ready to collect *them*.

'Cancel the car,' Mikael said.

Cursing, he reloaded his briefcase and headed out to his car, making light work of the dark city streets. At the hotel he tossed his keys at the valet and made his way up to the twenty-fourth floor— only to meet Layla, stepping into the elevator as he came out.

'Where do you think you're going?'

'I am looking for my driver...'

Mikael tried not to notice how gorgeous she looked in a tight red dress, and he also tried not to recall how soft her feet were as he saw that she had managed to get the shoes in her size.

Then he looked at black eyes that were almost crossing as they tried to focus.

'You're drunk!' Mikael accused.

'Am I?' Layla said, sounding very pleased with herself.

'No way are you going out tonight,' Mikael said, frogmarching her back to her suite.

'You can't stop me.'

'I'll call your brother, then,' Mikael said. 'Because *I'm* not going to police you.'

He pulled out his phone the second they got into her suite. There were glasses everywhere, and dresses and shoes; it was clear that Layla was seriously going all out for her week of fun.

'You will *not* call Zahid!' Layla roared. 'I am an adult. I am capable of making my own decisions.'

'Fine, then,' he snapped. 'But I'm warning you: it would be beyond foolish for you to go out in that state, but if you choose to then that's up to you.' He turned to leave and yet he couldn't. 'Where exactly are you planning to go tonight?'

'I want to go to a club—to dance.'

'With...?' Mikael looked at her and tried to ignore her gorgeousness, tried to be cross. And yet he was tempted to laugh. What did she do to his head? 'Have you got any money, Layla?'

'No.'

'Have you any idea of the trouble you could get into?'

She just looked at him, and suddenly it was very easy for Mikael to be cross—just not with her.

'My current client isn't the only bastard out there, Layla.'

'Mikael…'

'No, you need to hear this.'

'Mikael, help me!'

He watched her beautiful face pale and her hand clutch her throat.

'I think…' Layla said. 'I think that I'm…'

He got her to the bathroom just in time.

Never in his life had he done this, and never again would he do this, but Mikael stood holding her silky black hair as she knelt in the bathroom.

'I *should* ring your brother, you know.'

'I know,' she said. Unseen by her, Mikael smiled as she continued, 'But you won't.'

Yes, he really should ring Zahid and have him come and collect her—but instead he ran her a bath as he thought about her brother.

Mikael had been worried—and with good reason. Zahid must be beside himself.

Mikael was not a sentimental person—not in the least—but surely a text to put him at ease could not cause any harm?

As he waited for the bath to fill Mikael fired a quick text.

Just to let you know, Layla is fine.

'Have a bath and wash your hair, and then I suggest you get some sleep.'

'Can you send someone in to wash me?'

'*Wash* you?'

She had no idea how to do it herself.

'I'll tell you this much…' He was breathing very hard as he massaged shampoo with rather angry fingers into her hair. He'd insisted she keep her underwear on—as if that would go down well with the defence! 'You're completely—'

He'd been about to say *spoilt* but he halted and thought about it as he rinsed the shampoo out of her hair.

She might be pampered, and way too used to getting her own way, yet Layla was the most unspoiled person he had ever met.

'There,' Mikael said. 'Your hair's clean.'

'Jamila oils it now.'

'There,' Mikael said again, a little while later. 'Your hair is washed *and* conditioned and now...' he moved in to pull the plug and met her lovely feet again '...I'll help you out of the bath. Then you're to dry yourself and put on a robe.'

'Okay.' For once she agreed.

He helped her out and she made sure that Mikael too was soaking as she toppled against him.

'I still feel a bit...' She didn't know how to describe it as he handed her a towel. 'I think I like you,' Layla said, and Mikael's jaw gritted as she continued. 'Not just *like* you...it feels a bit different to that...' She turned as he walked out. 'Where are you going?'

'To do some work,' he said. 'Work that pays in dollars instead of stones.'

He was cross, Layla realised as he stalked out. But lovely.

He didn't even look up as she came out of the bathroom.

'I know that I behaved badly tonight...it was just too enticing...' She looked out at the lights that still beckoned.

'You need to sleep,' Mikael said, 'and I need to work out what the hell I'm going to do with you.'

He didn't trust her as far as he could throw her—but not in a bad way.

Mikael went to the couch and took out his laptop and got to work as Layla made her way to the bedroom.

'The maids didn't put out a nightdress.'

Mikael closed his eyes for a second before answering. She was the most exhausting person he had ever met. 'Just sleep in your robe.'

'But it's damp.' She came out from the bedroom. 'If I sleep in damp clothes I'll catch a cold.'

'That's an old wives' tale.'

'I don't understand.'

Neither did Mikael, because a few minutes later he was naked from the waist up and trying not to notice just how long her legs were as she walked from the bathroom wearing his shirt and was finally safe in bed for the night.

'Mikael!' she called from the bedroom. 'Will you still take me out tomorrow night?'

Mikael didn't answer.

'Mikael…'

'Layla,' Mikael called back, 'could you really see checkmate?'

Silence.

'I want the truth—yes or no?'

'No.'

She started laughing and Mikael gave a wry smile. He'd add the extra twenty bloody minutes he'd spent staring at the board to her bill.

'Go to sleep, Layla.'

Finally she did as she was told and Mikael got on with his work, only pausing occasionally.

The sound of her soft snoring was actually quite relaxing…

CHAPTER SIX

LAYLA AWOKE TO the gorgeous scent of Mikael.

Or rather the gorgeous scent of Mikael's shirt, and she lay there remembering him bathing her and how cross but kind he had been. There was a flurry low in her stomach as she remembered toppling into him and smiling up at him, telling him that she liked him.

She still did.

Yes, he was a commoner, but she only had six days now and Mikael, Layla decided, would be her romance for the week.

Layla picked up the phone by the bed and ordered a thinly sliced apple, some mint tea and iced water and then padded out to the lounge, where Mikael was stretched out asleep on the sofa.

He looked so different asleep, Layla thought as she stood over him.

He appeared a lot less cross and he had shadows under his eyes like those Layla had had once had when she'd caught a cold. She looked at his chin. In all the photos she had seen he had been clean-shaven, but she loved his stubbly jaw.

Layla's eyes drifted from his face to his body, which was just as beautiful.

His skin was pale and his flat nipples were the same dark red as his lips. She liked his flat stomach, and she blew out a guilty breath as she saw the snake of hair that led from his navel. She knew she should not be looking there and so moved her eyes back to his face instead. She watched him wake, his grey eyes frowning into hers. A look of concern darted across his face.

'Good morning!' Layla smiled down at him.

'What time is it?' Mikael asked with a horrible, panicked feeling that he might have overslept.

'Sunrise!' Layla smiled again and then turned when there was a knock at the door. Mikael watched as a trolley was wheeled in.

'You've ordered breakfast?'

'No, just something to cleanse my palate—my mouth is very dry.'

'I bet it is,' Mikael said, watching as she nibbled on her apple while walking over to the window.

'It's beautiful,' Layla said, looking out at the Sydney skyline. The Opera House looked gold in the morning sun and the whole city was gleaming and beckoning. 'I'm trying to think what to do today.'

'I've already decided,' Mikael said, picking up her glass of sparkling water and draining it. 'You're joining me at work.' He'd decided that just before dozing off. 'You can sit in the public gallery.'

'Really?' Layla beamed. 'How exciting!'

'And you're to behave and be quiet.'

'I *do* know how to behave,' Layla retorted.

Mikael looked at that mane of black hair and those very long brown legs and tried not to wonder if she had panties on; instead he turned his mind to think about clothes for her. Dressed in the silver tunic she had arrived in, or any of the clothes she had bought last night, she would bring the court down!

'We need to tone you down, Layla.' Mikael stood and rang down to the desk, not caring who needed to be awoken in order to facilitate his request.

'Why do I need to be toned down?'

'Because you don't want your brother to find you… And anyway,' he told her, 'today it's *my* turn to shine.'

'Oh, Mikael…' Layla smiled. 'I cannot wait.'

A selection of outfits was brought to the suite for Layla to try, and Mikael ordered coffee too.

'I'm hungry,' Layla moaned, coming out of the bedroom in a navy shift dress and screwing up her nose.

Mikael was putting his shirt back on—it was still warm from her.

'We'll have breakfast out,' Mikael said, because he liked to eat at his favourite café during a trial and he was not changing his routine for Layla. 'That looks nice.'

'*You* wear it, then,' she said. 'It makes me feel miserable.'

She selected another outfit and headed back to the bedroom. The pale grey linen suit looked very drab to Layla, but when she put it on the skirt was nice and short, and with a silver cami and the jacket's sleeves rolled up she liked it.

'I'm ready,' she said, stepping out of the bedroom and putting on her silver jewelled slippers. 'And I'm very, *very* hungry, Mikael.'

There was no chance of outshining Layla, Mikael thought, because she looked stunning. 'Don't you want to do your make-up?' he asked—because wasn't that what *every* woman did?

She wasn't every woman, though…

Layla shook her head. 'I will only wear make-up for my future husband. Come on, Mikael, I need to eat soon or I will faint.'

'I won't be picking you up if you do,' he said.

Mikael's choice of café was a trendy converted warehouse that was frequented by his peers, who would all leave him alone, knowing that he wouldn't want small talk this morning or best wishes for the day.

'This is near the hotel where my brother and Trinity are,' Layla commented.

'Now do you see why I wanted you in different clothes?' Mikael said, and she nodded. 'Don't worry,' he added, 'even if we see them, you're having your week.'

Heads turned as they walked in. Not because Mikael was with a woman, more because Mikael was with a woman this close to the end of a trial—and what a woman she was!

Waving and smiling to anyone who caught her eye, Layla was surprised when they didn't wave back.

'Are you nervous about today?' Layla asked, but then the waiter handed her a menu. She looked at it for a moment and then handed it back to him. 'I can't read or write English,' she said, and beamed.

Mikael watched as Joel just about fell to the floor as she aimed her smile at him.

'I'll order,' Mikael said, because Joel would clearly be only too happy to go through the entire menu for her. 'Just fruit and pastries,' Mikael said, 'and two coffees—and two on sub. Actually, just a regular cappuccino for my guest,' he said, because he always had an extra shot, and a high-on-caffeine Layla he wasn't sure he could handle.

'You drink a lot of coffee,' she commented.

'Because I didn't get a lot of sleep last night,' he said, and then realised what she meant. He had ordered four coffees. 'Two are on sub...'

Mikael let out a breath as she frowned. Just one easy conversation where he didn't have to explain everything would be welcome, but that wasn't going to happen this century.

'If someone needs a coffee and they don't have any money then they can ask if there are any on sub.'

She still looked bemused.

'Do you have homeless people in Ishla?'

'I believe so, but my father refuses to discuss those sort of issues with me.'

Those sort of issues.

Mikael was less than impressed when she wrinkled up her nose.

'They're people, Layla,' Mikael said. He didn't order those coffees without reason. How much easier would *his* life have been had he been able to get a warm drink or a sandwich just by asking. For a long while Mikael had scrimped or scavenged for every morsel. He remembered that every time he ordered food, and he did not take kindly to some pampered princess screwing up her nose.

'Of course they are people,' Layla said, 'but it is an issue, no?' She shrugged her shoulders, but not in a dismissive way. 'I am not to worry about such things, apparently.'

She looked over to him and Mikael realised that again he had misread her when she spoke on.

'But I do.'

The coffee was lovely, Layla declared, thanking Joel profusely for the shake of chocolate on the top of her frothy milk. 'What an amazing combination,' Layla said, as if Joel himself had invented cappuccino.

'You didn't answer me before,' Layla said once Joel had gone. 'Are you nervous about today?'

'I'm never nervous,' Mikael said.

'Never?'

'No.' He shook his head. 'I'm *prepared* for today.'

'Good! So I will start my magical week listening to you in court. I'm looking forward to it *so* much.'

She wasn't being sarcastic, but Mikael took a second to realise it.

'Layla—' he started, because what had seemed the most sensible idea when he had fallen asleep in the small hours felt more than a touch uncomfortable now. 'Some of the things that I say today... some of the things you might hear..'

'It's fine!' she dismissed.

'It's really not fine...' He breathed out, for today he was going to discredit the deceased. Today was not a day during which Mikael would be endearing himself to anyone. But immediately Layla waved his concerns away.

'I've been following the trial. I know what he did.'

'What he's *accused* of doing,' Mikael corrected, but she just shrugged.

'He should be fed to the dogs!' she said, and then looked straight at him. 'And in my country that isn't just a saying.'

The whole café seemed to fall silent as the impossible happened.

Mikael Romanov laughed.

At seven a.m. near the end of a trial.

'So,' Mikael said as their breakfast was served, 'apart from dancing and getting drunk, what else is on your bucket list?' He chose to explain that before she asked him to. 'Your to-do list.'

'Oh…' Layla smiled. 'This.'

'What?'

'This is on my list—I wanted to share a meal in a restaurant with a sexy man. But in my plan it was in the evening and we were holding hands.'

'This is a café,' Mikael said, 'and I don't hold hands. What else?'

'I'm not telling you,' Layla said, popping blueberries in her mouth.

'Go on,' he pushed, 'tell me.'

'If you take me dancing tonight I will tell you some more.'

'I'm not dancing till the jury is in,' Mikael said, 'and if today goes well then you'll be long gone by then.'

'Then you won't ever find out.' Layla shrugged.

'How about dinner tonight?' he offered.

'Somewhere romantic?' Layla checked.

'I don't do romance.'

'Oh. Well.' She shrugged again. 'Your loss. I might have to find another person to fulfil my wishes.'

When they arrived at chambers a rather bemused Wendy took Layla over to the court while Mikael showered and changed into a fresh suit, and then he sat for a long quiet hour going through everything in his mind, over and over. He scratched out phrases, honed in on words, re-examined every angle, just to plant that seed of beyond reasonable doubt.

As court resumed Mikael glanced up at the public gallery just once to check that she was there.

She was smiling down at him.

In black robes and a wig Mikael looked even

more incredible than he had when he had been on her computer.

His voice, when finally he commenced his closing argument, had the goosebumps rising on Layla's arms, for it was rich and deep and reached every corner of the courtroom. It was her privilege to sit, absolutely mesmerised, as Mikael set to work.

On many occasions throughout the long day Mikael rather wished that Layla had left, for what he had to say was not pretty.

There was a furious audible gasp from the gallery as he reminded the jury of a witness's testimony—an ex-boyfriend of the deceased had stated that she preferred her sex rough.

God, no wonder he was loathed by so many, Mikael thought as the lights in court seemed to flicker as social media lit up, demanding that Romanov's guts should be hated.

Still he did not look up to the public gallery.

'My client has never denied that intercourse took place before the deceased fell in the stairwell,' Mikael said. 'Nor has he denied that the sex was violent. But that was by mutual consent.'

Still he did not look up—even when the judge called for someone to be removed from the public gallery for shouting obscenities at Mikael.

He pointed to the gallery once, though, as order was restored. 'Up there is emotion,' he reminded the jurors. 'Down here we examine facts.'

The court broke for lunch and Layla hoped he would come and find her, so that she could tell him how well he was doing, but he was nowhere to be seen.

'Where's Mikael?' Layla asked Wendy, who was walking towards her.

'He just texted me and asked if I would take you to lunch.'

'Oh.'

'What would you like to eat?' Wendy asked as they stood in a café, and Layla frowned. It was so much easier with Mikael.

'What that man is eating,' Layla said.

'A burger?'

Layla nodded.

'With the lot?' Wendy checked.

Layla had no idea what she meant, but nodded.

Despite the company, it was possibly the best meal of Layla's life—and then it was back to court to watch Mikael at his savage best.

'My client has freely admitted that he was angry she had stayed out so late, and that she was drunk when she got home and an argument ensued. Arguments happen—so does make-up sex.'

The lights flickered again.

Hour by hour he shredded the prosecution's arguments, twisted words, questioned statements of so-called fact, reminded the jury of the amount of alcohol and drugs involved, inching them towards *his* conclusion.

'Did she ask the paramedics to get him away from her?' Mikael demanded. 'Did she plead with the treating doctors and nurses to keep this monster away? No, she did not. In fact, as we heard from the senior nurse who took her to the operating theatre where she subsequently died, she *asked* to see her boyfriend.'

Mikael watched as a couple of jurors frowned.

'Does that sound like a woman in abject ter-ror? Does that sound like a woman who had been raped and beaten in a stairwell to you?'

Mikael was the second most hated man in Aus-tralia today.

His client was the first.

But for Igor he delivered the best defence he knew how.

CHAPTER SEVEN

MIKAEL WAS UNSURE of his reception when he knocked on Layla's hotel room door a few hours after Wendy would have delivered her back there.

'You were fantastic!' Layla opened the door, her smile beaming. She was back in her red dress and sparkly shoes. 'Oh, my, Mikael—you almost had me!'

'Almost?' he checked.

'That bastard is as guilty as hell but, *wow*, you were amazing!'

'You're the strangest woman I have ever met.'

'I was hoping to see you close up in your robes and wig. Why didn't you meet me for lunch?'

'Layla…' He was about to point out that it was only by some miracle that he'd even remembered she had no money and would have no idea what to do for lunch and so had contacted Wendy, but he left it.

He was relieved by her reception.

Pleased, even.

Layla had been right. He did not care what others thought of him—not a single bit.

He had today.

It was a relief not to have to justify himself.

'How was lunch?' Mikael asked instead.

'I had a burger with the lot and it was fantastic. Wendy isn't much fun, though, is she?'

'Wendy is an incredibly busy woman and it was nice of her to give up her lunch for you.'

'Give up her lunch?' Layla frowned. 'But she ate more than I did.'

She looked at Mikael; he was so very handsome. and she liked it when he smiled—which he was now. Layla knew it was rare, and that he was not a very happy person, and she loved the light it brought to his eyes.

'So what now?' she asked.

'We wait for the verdict.'

'I mean what happens *now*?'

'Do you want to go out for dinner?'

'Pardon?' Layla smiled.

'Would you like to go out somewhere nice for dinner.'

'Somewhere *romantic*,' Layla corrected. 'Yes, please, Mikael.'

He took her to a waterside restaurant. Yes, the view was to die for, and usually he would have asked for a table outside, but tonight their only view would be of each other, and he asked for their most intimate table.

'This is lovely,' Layla said as she slipped in to her side of a velvet booth. 'Oh, our knees are touching!'

'Better?' Mikael asked, moving his.

'No,' she said, because she'd liked the feel of his knees near hers. When he moved them back she smiled. '*That's* better.'

'Do you want wine?'

'I want champagne,' Layla said. 'The best one.'

'Of course you do.'

'Do you have any cigarettes?'

'I don't smoke,' Mikael said, reading the menu, 'and neither do you.'

'I'd like to try a joint.'

'Layla!'

'Zahid nearly got expelled from school when one was found in his locker, and since then I have wanted to try. Just one time.'

'It's illegal.'

'I know a very good defence lawyer!' Layla said, and her knees nudged his.

'You do!'

'Do you have a girlfriend?' Layla asked as the champagne was poured. Mikael declined; he only drank water when he was in the midst of a trial.

'I have girlfriends.'

'Anyone serious?'

'If there was then she wouldn't be very pleased right now.'

'It's just a romantic dinner,' Layla said, and closed her eyes in bliss as she tasted her first champagne.

'If you wanted romance then you chose the wrong man.'

'Why?'

'Because I'm not interested in romance,' he said, and then changed the subject. 'So, apart from drunken debauchery, what else is on your list?'

'I just want to kiss, to flirt, to be sent flowers— and then I will return and marry and be content that I had one magical week.'

He stared at her. It didn't seem an awful lot to ask, and he loathed the lengths she had had to go to and the very real trouble she might find her- self in.

Serious trouble.

'I would like to spend a day in bed.'

'Layla,' he said. 'You can't go around saying that.'

'I'm only saying it to you…' She frowned at his concern. 'Always I have duties, and if I don't have duties then I am to join my father for breakfast or have my hair braided. I just want one day where there is nothing planned.'

He rolled his eyes as he realised her statement had been completely innocent. 'I apologise,'

Mikael said. 'I thought when you said a day in bed...'

She thought that completely hilarious. 'I wasn't talking about *sex*! Don't worry, Mikael, I'm not going to do anything reckless—I know I have to return to Ishla intact...'

'Are we really having this conversation?'

'We are.' She smiled and looked at the purple marks that were still under his eyes. 'You look as if *you* could use a day in bed,' she said, 'for sleeping.'

'Well, that's not going to happen any time soon.' Mikael gave a thin smile. 'But once the verdict is in I'm going to have some time away.'

'On your yacht!' Layla said. 'With your blonde women!'

'You really did do your homework, didn't you?'

'I told you that I did.' She shrugged. 'So, how long do you think the jury will take?'

'As long as they take.'

'I loved watching you today...' she admitted. 'I kept hoping that you would look up.'

'I had other things on my mind.'

Now he had only Layla, and when her fingers nudged his Mikael took them.

'How is your game of chess going?' she asked, and they both smiled at her previous teasing.

'Can you play?' he asked.

'I am very good,' Layla said. 'I play with my father when he has the time, and often myself, but now I also play it online. It's fun—there is always someone in the world to play with and very often I win. Perhaps I could beat you?'

He saw the challenge in her eyes.

'Perhaps you could,' he said, 'if I had a migraine.'

Layla laughed. 'Don't dismiss me,' she warned.

And then she said something that meant he could not dismiss her—for it made them the same.

'I get bored a lot in Ishla, though it is better now that I can teach…' She gave a little smile. 'And now that I have a computer!'

Bored.

Mikael took her other hand and looked down at their entwined fingers to steady himself just for a moment. That word he could more than relate to.

He recalled his years on the streets—hour after hour to fill with nothing.

Day after interminable day.

He did not remind her that she was privileged, he did not scold her with his eyes, for with that word she had him.

Mikael looked into her black eyes and saw the dance behind them, the intelligence that stretched beyond the world she'd been born to.

'Are you nervous about going back to Ishla?' he asked.

'No,' Layla said. 'I will be in trouble when I return—I accept that—but trouble always settles. I love my family,' she said, 'and I feel sorry that I have had to upset them to get what I want, but there was no other way.'

His hands were warm and dry and his fingers moved to the tiny scar on her otherwise flawless skin.

'What happened there?' Mikael asked.

'When we were nine Hussain, my future husband, showed me how to make a match burn twice.'

'Do you love him?'

'I don't know him,' Layla said. 'We played as children. I get to choose my husband, but I have been told, for the good of Ishla, that Hussain would be the wisest choice. My heart does not think so, though.'

He wanted to lift her wrist and kiss it better. Mikael had never felt anything like it before. But then Layla got too close.

'What are your family like?' she asked.

'I don't have any family.'

'Are your parents dead?'

Her question was so clinical he was able to answer.

'I don't know.' He didn't elaborate; instead he dropped hands and took up the menu, started to read out the choices, but she halted him.

'You choose for me,' she said. 'I want what you order—I want to try your favourite thing.'

'Is there anything you especially like or dislike?'

'I want to try whatever.'

So Mikael ordered for them. He taught her how

to peel the fattest, plumpest prawns and their fingers played together in the warm water bowl.

'I love these,' Layla said. 'I want to eat prawns again.'

'Don't you have them in Ishla?'

'I don't know,' she said. 'I must ask my father to get some for me.'

Mussels, oysters—all were bliss. But Layla just wanted more prawns.

'I could live off these,' she said, and then very rapidly changed the subject back to where she wanted it to be. 'How can you not know if your parents are dead or alive? Can't you trace them?'

'Leave it, Layla.'

'But I want to know.'

'Well, I don't want to tell you.' Mikael refused to reveal anything. 'What do you want for dessert?'

'Prawns.'

After a draining black day it was a lovely night, and as he dropped her off at the hotel Mikael did the right thing: gave the valet his keys for a short while and saw her to her door.

'Aren't you staying tonight?' she asked as they approached her suite.

'I hope there's no need for me to stay,' Mikael said. 'Unless you're planning on going out again?'

'No,' she said. 'There is no need for me to go out tonight. I have had the best day and the best night of my life and I am feeling very content.'

'Good.'

'Well, almost the best day,' Layla said. 'But it would be even better if you kissed me.'

'I don't think that's wise,' he said.

'One kiss.' She smiled, swiping her door pass. 'Anyway, you have to leave me your shirt to wear—I still don't have a nightdress.'

'Your brother asked me to—'

'You don't have to keep my promises for me,' Layla interrupted. 'I shall be returning to Ishla a virgin.'

'We were talking about a kiss!'

'So what's the problem, then?' Layla said.

She soon found out.

Mikael turned her around to face him and it was a little like being in the car, with him trying to put on her seatbelt. Every touch had her awareness heightened. She stood shivering in anticipation as he positioned them. She felt his hand on her shoulder and his face move to hers, and then she was lost—because nothing in her imaginings could have prepared her for those arrogant lips turned tender.

His kiss was very soft at first, and one hand rested on her waist, the other at her shoulder.

Then she felt the slip of his tongue and the slide of his hand to the back of her head. She had not known that tongues kissed too. It was shocking, it was sensual, it was the gateway to paradise—and her hands went to his hair now as she matched his tongue. And then, whether it was his hand on her bottom or just the call of her groin, they moved in closer and *that* was the problem—one kiss led to more.

She could feel him hard at her centre, but more than that she could feel the strain of her breasts and the pull low in her stomach as Mikael kissed her ever deeper and then pulled his head back.

One kiss and her chin was red and her lips swollen.

'I'd better shave next time,' he said.

'We agreed one kiss.' Layla smiled. 'But now I know why it is trouble…'

He released her. 'I'd better go.'

'You need to leave my nightdress,' she said. 'Are you working tomorrow?'

'I am,' he said, 'but I'll try and finish early.' He was worried about her going out without him, but at the same time didn't want to curtail her. 'What are you doing tomorrow?'

'I have a very special day planned,' Layla said as he took off his shirt and handed it to her. 'I am not getting out of bed.'

'Oh?' Mikael waited for her to elaborate but she had clearly said all she wanted to on the subject.

She looked at him, naked from the waist up, and wanted more of what she had so recently felt. 'Can you kiss me now, so I can feel your skin?'

'Definitely not,' he said, putting on his jacket and pocketing his tie. 'Night, Layla.'

'I have another thing on my bucket list now,'

Layla said as he headed for the door. 'I want to have an orgasm.'

'I'm going home.'

'Seriously, Mikael.' She saw him to the door. 'I thought you could only achieve orgasm with sexual intercourse, and even then only if you were lucky. Am I wrong?'

'Very wrong!' Mikael almost groaned. 'Goodnight, Layla.'

CHAPTER EIGHT

LAYLA AWOKE LONG after sunrise and lay in bed for a happy hour, just remembering Mikael's kiss and replaying it over and over, before ringing down for breakfast—only to find out that it was lunchtime.

'What would you like, Layla?' The staff thought she was wonderful, and the head chef was brought to the phone to help her with her order.

'I want someone to come and help me put on the television, and I want a thinly sliced and peeled apple to cleanse my palette, and then something nice to eat.'

'Such as?'

'Sweet,' Layla said. 'Some fruit. You choose for me. One other thing—can I get a joint from you?'

'No.'

'Okay, just some sweet milk to drink, then.'

Apart from when she had caught that cold from wearing damp clothes Layla had never spent a day in bed before, and she intended to enjoy it.

The maids delivered her food and Terrence, the butler, gave her a tutorial on the television's remote control, and Layla lay in bed, still in Mikael's shirt, dipping raspberries in white chocolate sauce and drinking milk laced with cinnamon and nutmeg while watching television.

It was fantastic!

She watched as the couple on the screen started kissing, and blew out her breath as she remembered her kiss last night with Mikael again.

She watched, eyes wide, as the man started to take off the woman's top, and started to blush as he undid her bra.

Oh!

Layla knew that she should not be watching this, that she should turn it off, but she could not stop herself. She wanted some lemonade from the fridge. Usually she would use the phone to get Terrence to fetch it for her, but she did not want to be disturbed and so, with her eyes not leaving the screen, for the first time Layla fetched a drink for herself.

The couple were now on the bed, with a sheet over them, and Layla just about choked on her lemonade at the noises they were making. She reached for the phone—not to call down to the desk, though; instead she called Mikael.

'I can't speak now, Layla,' he said. 'I'm about to have a meeting with my client's family.'

'Just one question?' she begged.

'One.'

'I am watching television and I think people are having sex in the middle of the day and they are not married to each other.'

'You're not watching television, then,' he said. 'You've put on the adult channel.'

God, he thought, another thing he'd have to have removed from her bill before her brother saw it.

'Oh!'

He heard her gasp of disappointment. 'Now they are putting on the thing where they try to make me thirsty again.'

'That's a commercial.' He laughed. Okay, so she

wasn't on the adult channel. 'Do you know the name of the show that you're watching?'

Layla told him.

'That's what we call a soap,' Mikael explained. 'They're not really having sex—they're just acting.'

'Well, it's very good acting,' Layla said. 'She looks how I felt when you kissed me last night. Are they dressed beneath the sheet?'

'I would think so.'

'But I saw the top of his bottom.'

'I have to go.' Mikael hesitated as Wendy buzzed. 'Hold on a moment, Layla.'

She would happily hold on, she thought—her show was back on and the couples were lying together and smiling.

'I really do have to go, Layla.'

'Just one more question…' She didn't get to ask it.

'Layla, the jury's returning.'

'So soon? But—'

Mikael had already hung up.

He met with his client, who was sweating. 'It's not good that they're back so soon, is it?'

'No,' he said.

'A little bit of hope would be nice.'

He did not respond. He had done his very best for the filth that now sat next to him. What hope had he given his victim that night?

Mikael sat, his face impassive, waiting.

'All rise.'

Mikael did.

Layla hopped on one leg as she watched the court reporter on the court's steps and Terrence stood beside her, navigating social media and giving her updates.

'The verdict's coming.'

'Oh,' Layla said. 'Do you think he'll be upset if he loses?'

'He rarely loses,' Terrence said. 'Probably…' Terrence paused. 'Okay, here it is…' He paused for a moment and then read out the verdict. 'Guilty.'

Layla gasped as pandemonium hit the courtroom.

'They're shouting abuse from the public gallery,' Terrence said, reading from a laptop as

Layla watched the news. 'The judge is thanking the jury.'

'What are they saying about Mikael?' Layla demanded.

Nothing the court reporter or Terrence could find gave her a clue as to how he was feeling.

Mikael Romanov, the court reporter said, was, as always, a closed book.

Not even later, as he walked down the court steps and ignored the reporters, did his expression give Layla an inkling as to his thoughts.

'Send someone to tidy the room,' Layla said, 'and I want more fruit and chocolate sauce and champagne...' Rapid were her orders.

'Champagne?' Terrence checked. 'I don't think he'll be in the mood for celebrating.'

'*Now*, Terrence, please!'

Mikael's expression was unreadable as he walked back to chambers—just as it would have been had his client been found not guilty.

No one could ever guess what went on in his mind.

He de-robed and took a long drink of sparkling water. Then, a short while later, his car gunned from the car park and Mikael left in a puff of smoke, driving straight to the hotel, where he threw his keys at the valet and this time told him to park it. He took the elevator to her door.

'Enter,' Layla called, and he took out his swipe card and let himself in.

She was sitting up in bed, still wearing his shirt. There was champagne in a bucket and he hadn't had a drink in two months, and there was fruit and chocolate sauce. She understood him, Mikael realised, somehow she understood him—or rather she simply let him be.

'Are you upset?' Layla asked.

'No.'

'Because I thought you could just hide in bed with me. Not for sex. I have always dreamt of it, but today I found out it is really nice to sit in bed and just eat.'

'Okay...' Mikael's voice was a touch wary, but he took off his jacket and tie, shoes and socks, and then opened the champagne. He poured two glasses and joined her, but lay on top of the bed rather than getting in.

'How do you feel?' Layla asked, and Mikael thought for a moment before answering.

'Elated.' He turned and looked at her. 'There's no such thing as a bad day at the office for me, Layla. That bastard is going down for a very long time.'

He breathed out, stunned at his own honesty.

'Do you ever not try your best?' Layla's eyes narrowed as she asked a very brave question—one perhaps no one else would ever dare ask.

'I try my best for all my clients. I fight for them with everything I have.'

'Always?'

'Always,' Mikael said. 'And then, if they are found guilty, I know, as best I can know, that a guilty man has gone down.'

The champagne tasted nice, Mikael thought.

'Aren't you going to ask if it bothers me...?' He was surprised by the lack of the oh, so familiar question.

'Clearly it doesn't,' Layla said. 'I doubt many

people could get you to do something you did not want to do.'

'You did,' Mikael said. 'I took you on when I didn't want to.'

'Ah, but you were attracted to me,' she said, and dipped a raspberry in white chocolate sauce. 'Intrigued.'

'I was,' he said. 'It doesn't trouble you, then?'

'Of course not,' she said, and instead of eating the raspberry herself she fed it to him, liking the feel of his lips on her fingers and the wetness of his tongue so much that she did it again as she spoke on. 'For a system to work, both sides need to be represented well. In some lands there is no such system.'

'How does it work in Ishla?'

'If you are found guilty of a crime you are either pardoned, removed or killed.'

'You can be pardoned?'

'Of course. It is at my father's discretion and once you are pardoned there is no grudge, no stigma. If you cannot be fully pardoned then you are removed from society till you can be fully pardoned.' She looked over at him where he lay on the bed, silent. 'Why are you smiling?'

'That's what you do to me,' he admitted. Maybe it was because she was here just for a few days—just a transient timeframe—which meant he could let down his perpetual guard a touch.

'Did you always want to study law?'

'No.'

'Why did you?'

Mikael shook his head. His guard wasn't that low. 'It's just as well you don't read and write,' he said, pulling her into the crook of his arm. 'You'd be running for prime minister.'

'But I can read and write,' Layla said. 'Just not English. But I am going to learn—it will be good for my work.'

'You *work*?' This he had to hear!

'Of course—though I don't get paid for it. My father was concerned because although the girls in Ishla were receiving an education their grades were far lower than the boys. We had a discussion and decided that I would speak with them once a month and encourage them. Now I speak to all the classes. Every day I have students, but I cannot know all their names. Their grades are improving,' Layla said. 'I'm very good at it and they love me.'

'You're modest too.'

She shrugged. 'I loathe false modesty. I tell my girls to be proud of themselves and their achievements.'

They drank more champagne in silence.

Sometimes she felt his mouth on her hair; sometimes she felt his fingers stroke her forearm. It was the most peaceful Layla had ever felt. He dozed, and she liked the thump-thump of his heart in her ear, liked the rise and fall of his chest, and she liked the view too—because she could see the outline of what had been pressing into her last night.

'What are you doing?' Mikael asked as her fingers moved to undo the bottom part of his shirt.

'I want to see the hairy bit beneath your navel again,' she said, but his hand moved hers away and held it and she watched with a smile as the outline widened and stretched.

'What made you want to study law?' she asked again.

'You're persistent, aren't you?'

'Very, very persistent.' Layla nodded. 'I always get my own way in the end, so it would be much easier on you to just give in now.'

It was tell her or let her hand go.

Speak or find her mouth.

Mikael knew what he would prefer, but she had invited him to her bed 'not for sex', and it had been the nicest hiding place he had ever had.

He couldn't even be bothered to put the news on and find out what was being said.

Okay, he'd tell her why he had studied law.

Some of it.

'When I grew up I had no family. I just remember a flat and lots of people, but there was no one there that I called a parent. There were other children and lot of fights, drinking. One night everyone was moved on and I started to live on the streets.'

'As a beggar?'

'And a thief,' Mikael said. 'When I was around

twelve, maybe thirteen—I don't know exactly how old I was—a government worker helped me. His wife was dead and he took me in. I shared his home with him and his son, I got an identity, an assumed date of birth, and I went to school. I was always Mikael, but I took his surname.'

'What was it?'

'Igor Romanov,' Mikael said.

'He adopted you?'

'No,' Mikael said. 'I just took the surname. I was grateful to him, and worked very hard at school, but I still got into a lot of trouble. I was very angry. But when I got the gold medal at school Igor suggested law.'

Layla lay there trying to imagine a life without her family. She missed her mother every day, and even though she had never met her she knew so much about her.

Imagine not knowing anything…

Mikael lay in the dark place in his mind that he didn't visit very often.

How he had fought to survive in a world where no one had cared if he lived.

Worse than that, though, had been the boredom—hour after hour to fill.

Had he not had chess, Mikael knew that he would have lost his mind. Day in, day out, night in, night out, hour after hour, he would sit with men older than him who taught him so well he could soon beat them—until people had started to pay for a chance to play him.

They hadn't paid much, but it had been enough to feed him.

That was when Igor had stepped in, having heard about this boy who was being paid to play chess. Mikael had carried on playing, but there had been books then, and study, as Mikael had fast made up the years of education he had lost on the streets.

Layla's persistent fingers had slid into the gap between his shirt buttons and now idly stroked the hair there. He went to move them, but from her breathing and the sudden stillness of her fingers he realised she was sleeping.

Mikael lay and watched the sun set over Sydney as the tension of the past few months receded.

'Layla…' He felt her stir, and despite having washed her hair himself he could still smell the exotic scent when she moved. 'Would you like to go out?'

'Out?' Her hand pulled away from his stomach. 'Dancing.'

She was off the bed in a moment, and peeling off his shirt as she headed to the bathroom. Mikael had never known anybody get dressed so quickly.

'I've never danced,' she said excitedly as she pulled on her glittery shoes. 'What if I can't do it?'

'Oh, I'm sure you'll manage,' he said, ringing down for a driver and preparing to head out into the world instead of locking himself in for the night.

The trial was over; it was time for some fun.

CHAPTER NINE

HE CHOSE A very private, exclusive club, but as the driver dropped them off there was still a line-up for the less than perfect. They lifted the rope as soon as Mikael approached—but not before Layla had already bypassed the line.

She wasn't deliberately flouting the rules, Mikael realised, they had just never applied to her.

'I want to sit at the bar,' she said as they were led to a table.

'Fine,' Mikael said, because it was her night.

'I want to order.'

'Do so, then.'

'What do you want to drink?' she asked.

'They know my order,' he said

'A drink for Mikael and one Irish coffee for me.'

He just looked at the barman who, to his credit, only blinked once.

'Can I have some money to pay him, Mikael?' she asked.

'I have an account here.'

'I want to pay, though,' she said. 'I want to buy you a drink.'

With *his* money!

'Mikael!' A couple of silks came over. 'Didn't expect to see you here tonight. Bad luck—really thought you'd got him off.'

'So did I for a while,' Mikael said.

They chatted about work for a few moments, but all eyes were on Layla.

'Where the hell did you find *her*?'

'Don't ask.'

'She's stunning.'

'She's exhausting,' he said, and looked over to where Layla sat perched on a bar stool. She was wearing a cream moustache and chatting to the now besotted barman, who'd been foolish enough to say that he'd noticed her shoes as she came in.

'And now...' Layla smiled to the barman '...I take them dancing. Come on, Mikael!'

She *could* dance!

'It's so easy!' She beamed. 'So sexy!' She laughed. 'No wonder it is forbidden.'

As she danced and swayed Layla had possibly never been happier in her life, and her exuberance and sheer joy were infectious. So much so that the mood at the rather staid club lifted and a night that might have been spent commiserating over Mikael's loss seemed to have turned into a party—everyone was up and dancing.

'*You* are sexy, Mikael,' Layla said, wrapping her arms around his neck.

He was so lithe and so full of surprises—for she'd thought he would sit at the bar, but instead they'd moved together and danced into the small hours.

'Will you kiss me again?'

'Not here,' he said, and as the music slowed she leant against him.

'When we get back to the hotel can we do what they did on the television?'

Mikael frowned. It seemed a very, very long time ago since he'd been told that the verdict was in, and only when Layla spoke on did he remember she'd been watching a TV show.

'Can we act as if we're having sex but keep our panties on?' Layla asked.

'No,' Mikael said. 'And I don't wear panties.'

'Please?'

'No,' he said again.

'I'm tired of dancing now.' Layla sulked.

'Good.'

The driver took them back to the hotel.

'Thank you for taking me dancing.' She looked at him. 'Will you stay here with me tonight?'

Mikael had been thinking about the same thing all the car ride back to the hotel. 'Well, I've just had a chat with my self-control and, yes, I will stay here with you tonight.'

'Where are you going?' Layla said as they stepped into her suite and Mikael headed straight for the bathroom.

'To shave,' he said. Because she bruised like a peach and the kiss he wanted to give her would have her face in shreds.

Layla sat on the edge of the bath as Mikael

rolled up his shirtsleeves, went through the hotel tray and then rubbed shaving cream in his jaw.

'I think I sweated,' she said.

Mikael shook his head a little at her way with words.

'I would like another bath.'

'Run it yourself, then.'

She met his eyes in the mirror and held his gaze, and the look between them seemed to go on for ever.

'Did you enjoy dancing?' he asked.

'Very much,' she said, 'but not as much as our kiss.'

Without another word she stood and turned. She put in the bath plug and added oils as if she was making a very complicated recipe, and Mikael tried to concentrate on shaving as she started to undress.

Off came the red dress.

Then she slipped off her shoes.

The razor hovered at a safe distance as Layla took off her bra and he saw her pert breasts and dark swollen nipples.

Her panties were next, and Mikael rinsed his face for a very long time. But even with his eyes closed all he could see was the silky straight triangle of hair.

He checked in again with his self-control as Layla spoke.

'Can you wash me again?'

'I think you can do that yourself.'

'I am sure that I can,' she said, 'but I like it when you do it.'

She did.

She wanted to be kissed by him again and she wanted the feel of his arms and the touch of his naked skin. Mikael turned around and she looked at him, wanted to see more of him.

'Can you remove your shirt?'

He did, and he was more beautiful than he had been asleep on the sofa because now he was awake, and she saw the stretch of muscles as he removed it. Her eyes did not guiltily jerk upwards from the snake of ebony hair this time; instead they moved down, and it was very clear that what she was feeling was matched by Mikael.

'You could take the rest of your clothes off,' she invited.

'I don't think so,' Mikael said, because someone had to stay in control here and he guessed it would have to be him.

'I ache from dancing.'

'Ache no more,' he said, kneeling down.

Mikael washed her far more slowly than Jamila did. First he washed her neck and shoulders, and Layla closed her eyes in bliss at the feel of his fingers soaping her and the sound of him breathing.

Then he washed her arms, and it tickled a bit as he lifted one and soaped her. And then her breath caught as his hand soaped her breasts, one at a time and very slowly. Layla could feel her aching nipples and she looked down to where they were swollen and stretched. Her head was so heavy she rested it on his shoulder and started to kiss his neck.

His neck tasted wonderful, almost as nice as his mouth, and whatever he was doing with her breasts had her hungry to taste him some more.

'Move your mouth lower,' Mikael warned. 'If I have to face your brother it's going to be hard enough looking him in the eye without—'

He didn't finish, and Layla didn't really get what he meant, but as she pulled back she saw the red mark her mouth had made. She moved her deep kisses to his shoulder, licking, sucking and relishing the feel of her wet naked skin against his.

Mikael massaged her aching calves, and then his hand moved between her thighs.

'Jamila hands me a cloth for down there,' Layla said.

'Do you want a cloth?'

'No,' she said, but she was very honest as his fingers explored her intimate lips. 'Just touch me on the outside, though. I will be examined when I return.'

Mikael hated the thought of her being examined but said nothing.

With his free hand he lifted her mouth from his neck and kissed her as he had wanted to since the verdict had come in.

Layla felt the fierce passion of his mouth, the

untamed desire of his tongue, even as his fingers stayed gentle. His tongue did to her mouth what she wanted his fingers to do. She was clinging onto his head, squeezing his hand with her thighs, urging him as he resisted. He worked her clitoris and her mouth, holding on himself as he felt her mounting tension.

'Mikael—' She pulled her lips back in panic, but he smothered her protests with his mouth, and she held onto his shoulders as *something* rippled through her, warmer than the water she bathed in and yet it made her shiver. Her thighs clamped around his hand and still he stroked her—and a shocked Layla came for the first time to his hand as Mikael fought to stay gentle.

He stopped kissing her and she rested her head on his shoulder as the *something* receded and a new calm invaded her.

'I think I *did* have a seizure that time,' she said. 'Oh, Mikael, did you have an orgasm too?'

'Layla...' he warned, because her questions were at times so very direct. But he was laugh-

ing as he picked her up out of the bath and took
her to the bed.

'I can't touch with my hand what is not my husband's, but I want to see it.'

'Well, you're not going to,' he said. 'We're already heading into very dangerous territory.'

'Please, Mikael!'

'Layla, everyone has limits, and you're close to
exceeding mine.'

'You will sleep in the bed with me, though?'

'Yes,' he said. Preferably with a padlock on his
belt. 'I'm going to have a shower and then I'll be
in.'

'Bring me your shirt.'

He was gone quite a time and Layla lay smiling
until he came out. His trousers were back on and
he had forgotten to bring his shirt out.

'Sleep naked,' Mikael said when she asked him
to retrieve it. He was already climbing into bed.
'Live a little.'

'I'll catch a cold.'

'I'll keep you warm.'

It felt very nice to be against him, to feel his

hand stroking her ribcage and to rest her head on his chest.

'Did you like your verdict party?' she asked.

'Was that what it was?'

'Yes.'

How much easier would his job be if he came home to *her* at the end of a trial? Mikael thought, and then halted himself—because he didn't like to think that way.

He was tired now. And maybe he was relaxed from the shower, or maybe it was because soon she'd be gone, but when she asked a question so pertinent, instead of evading it or changing the subject, he answered with the truth.

'Where is Igor now?' she asked. 'Do you still keep in touch?'

'No,' Mikael said. 'Just after I finished school Igor was shot and killed.'

'Why?' She went to lift her head, but his hand held her body down just a fraction and she chose to stay still, because he was answering her questions now.

'Street court,' Mikael said.

'Street court?'

'A woman with a very prominent husband was having an affair. One day her husband came home and nearly caught them, but the man escaped through the bedroom window. She confessed that she had been having an affair and her husband pushed her to name her lover. She and Igor had worked together for years, and the husband was furious and had him killed.' Mikael was silent for a long time. 'All the evidence pointed to Igor: the wife had confessed and named him, the husband had known they were friends. And yet, despite so much evidence, Igor was *not* sleeping with her.'

'You know that for sure?'

'I do know that for sure—because the person leaving her bedroom was me. I had met her at Igor's work.'

'She named *Igor*?' Layla was appalled. 'Why would she do that when it wasn't even him?'

'Because she knew what would happen—she knew that her husband would have him killed and she did not want to lose a good screw.'

His voice was so bitter that Layla shivered, and even if she had never heard that word before she knew what he meant. She lay there as Mikael continued speaking.

'I hate her more than the man who shot him. I hate her so much that when a witness comes on the stand I picture her and I tear through their answers. I make sure, if they lie, that I expose it on the stand.'

'This is why you believe in a good defence?' Layla asked.

'Absolutely.'

'So how did you get to Australia?'

'Demyan,' Mikael said. 'He's a friend of mine. I grew up with him but he had moved to Australia. I knew there would soon be a bullet with my name on it, so I called him and his aunt helped me get to Australia.'

Mikael got out of bed and went to get a drink. He did not want her shock and sympathy; he did not want the questions and the prolonged conversation afterwards.

He had told her—wasn't that enough?

'The woman you hate…?' Layla asked, and Mikael gave a wry smile, because she could easily don a wig and robe, so perceptive were her questions. 'Did you love her also?'

'Almost,' he said. 'Well, it was the closest I've ever…' He took a belt of his drink and then a very deep breath, wondering if Layla would notice his hesitation—because the way he had felt in the past didn't come close to the way he was feeling right now.

Not that she would notice.

She was putting on her shoes in bed and admiring her long legs—but what he didn't know was that it was for *his* sake.

She'd sensed that he no longer wanted to talk.

He had never met anyone like her. Mikael was far more used to women pleading for conversation, for emotion, for him to just open up a touch more.

Layla had had all three without even asking.

And the only thing opening up now was her knees as Layla offered a rather appealing distraction from his very dark thoughts.

'Can you kiss me down there?'

It would, Mikael decided, be his absolute pleasure.

CHAPTER TEN

MIKAEL WOKE TO the sound of Layla ordering her usual thinly sliced and peeled apple with mint tea and water.

'And coffee,' Mikael said. 'And cake.'

'Cake?' Layla frowned.

'Cake,' he said.

'Could we have some chocolate cake and coffee too?' Layla said to the chef. 'And I would like my slice of cake just a little bit warm, with lots of cream to pour over it.' She ended the call and gave Mikael a wide smile. 'I love this phone; it's just fantastic.'

'I thought you'd always be ringing down your orders in your palace?'

'No.' Layla shook her head. 'I just tell Jamila what I want and she gets it for me.'

'So Jamila's your maid?'

'My handmaiden,' Layla said. 'She has been with me since the day I was born.'

'Like a mum?'

'No!' She laughed at the very thought. 'You don't love servants...' Her face was suddenly serious. 'I do feel a bit sick, though, at the moment when I think of her. She will be so worried. Oh, poor Jamila!'

'Sounds a lot like love to me,' Mikael said.

'So,' Layla asked, 'now that the trial is over, do you get that time off you talked about?'

He gave a wry smile. His work had barely begun. There would be sentencing, appeals... He closed his eyes at the thought of it all for a moment.

'I have a very busy day today. I have to meet with my client, his family.' God, Mikael knew where he'd rather be.

'That's fine. I am going to take a ferry and I am also going to do the Sydney Harbour Bridge climb.'

Mikael lay there and told himself that Layla was

twenty-four. She wasn't incapable. In fact she was possibly the cleverest person he had ever met...

And yet...

That gnawing of unease he had felt the first night when he had called the hotel to see what was happening was back.

It wasn't Layla so much who concerned him but others. She had been so protected it simply didn't enter her head that people might not be nice to her.

He closed his eyes as there was a knock at the door and tried to tell himself that he was overreacting, that of course she'd be fine out there without him.

Breakfast was delivered, along with something that Mikael was a bit embarrassed about now but had seemed a nice idea last night—there was a phone in the bathroom, after all...

'Flowers!' Layla was ecstatic 'And a card!' She opened it. 'What does it say?'

Mikael groaned. He'd forgotten in the moment when he'd ordered them that she couldn't read English, and now he'd have to read it out loud to her—but he waited till all the staff had gone.

'"*Layla, Thank you for an amazing end to a difficult day and an even more amazing night. Mikael.*"'

'No kisses?' Layla asked.

'Three.'

'Wow! Thank you! I will keep this for ever—maybe I hide it in my shoe or something, but I will find a safe place for it.'

'Layla, I don't want to get you in trouble...' Mikael halted. They were approaching the halfway mark of her week and four more nights were starting not to seem enough.

'Look, about today—'

'Mikael,' she interrupted, 'I want to have a day to myself. Please don't ask me to stay in the hotel.'

'Okay.' He pushed out a smile. 'You'll need some cash.'

'Yes, please.'

'Ask the hotel to organise a driver to take you wherever you want to go.'

'I'll be fine.'

'Take my number with you.'

She did.

She bought some white jeans and a top and some sandals from the boutique in the foyer, along with a handbag, and she was ready for her day of adventure.

Layla was worried that she might run into Trinity or Zahid, but at the same time she was determined that even if she did she would very simply refuse to return until her week was up.

She did not use the phone to organise a driver. Instead she decided to try taking a taxi again.

It was far easier the second time around, and she put on her seatbelt and understood that at the end she had to pay him.

Everything on her list Layla did.

She stood on the top of the bridge, being battered by the wind, and life felt so exhilarating that it was as if she were on the top of the world. Then she took a ferry to Manly and ordered a burger with 'the lot' and a can of lemonade, and she met some Dutch backpackers who were very serious but very lovely. They told her that she had to do the night-time harbour cruise while she was there.

'I don't know where to go,' she said.

'We'll show you.'

The cruise started long after sunset and went on for three magical hours. It was wonderful to see the Sydney skyline from the water at night. She could see the Opera House and the bridge all lit up. There was wine and a meal, though the prawns were not as nice as the ones she had had with Mikael, but she heard all the history—about Captain Cook and the convicts—and it was simply magical to sit with her new friends and listen, and feel the warm air on her skin.

She took a taxi back to the hotel, elated from a wonderful day out, tired and ready to have a bath and sleep. But as she opened her hotel door she jumped in surprise to see Mikael—and it was a Mikael that she had never seen before.

His face was grey and he did not return her smile when she walked in.

'Layla...' He was struggling to keep his voice even. 'Where have you been?'

'Doing the things on my list.' Layla smiled. 'I had a fantastic day."

'It's after midnight.'

'I did a cruise…'

'And you didn't think to call me?'

'Call you?' She frowned. 'You said to only call you in emergencies.'

Mikael had had a day like no other. The moment he had got to work he had changed his mind and called the room, only to find that she had already left.

He had got through his work as best he could but had then cleared his desk for the rest of the week, berating himself for leaving her alone.

It had been a very, *very* long night, and now there she stood, her hair whipped by the wind, her cheeks pink from too much sun. He pulled out his phone and fired a rapid text as, unknown to Layla, he had each night she'd been there—though never as late as it was this time.

Just to let you know, Layla is fine.

'Who are you texting at this time of night?'

'Your brother,' Mikael said. 'As I have every night.'

'Why would you do that?' she demanded.

'Because he cares about you, Layla.' Mikael was having great trouble not shouting. 'Because he must feel sick wondering just how the hell you are and whether or not you are safe, and a text—one bloody text—must surely help, just as one bloody phone call might have...'

He stopped himself. The relief he had felt as she'd walked through the door had flicked to anger and he was not used to it, for he had never really cared enough about another person, or been scared for them before.

'You have no idea the trouble you will have caused for me!' Layla roared. 'My brother will be furious that I am with a man this late at night.'

'Well, you should have thought of that,' he said. 'Did it never enter your head that I might be worried?'

It truly hadn't, and her eyes told him the same—which only incensed him even further. 'You, Layla, are the most selfish person I have ever met.'

'Selfish?' she shouted. 'How dare you call me selfish? I bought you a snowglobe.' She went to get it out of her bag, except Mikael was picking up his keys. 'Where are you going?'

'You've got a nerve to ask.'

'Mikael…'

He didn't answer. Instead he left, and she stood in the lovely suite alone.

She looked out to the dark sky and waited for him to come back.

And waited.

'Where are you Mikael?' she said to the streets below the hotel.

She loathed it. And she was starting to understand—because she wasn't scared for him, she just missed him, and she didn't like the row that had taken place. She was cross, too, for him texting Zahid—and yet she was starting to glimpse why he had.

Mikael was angry for about another twelve minutes and then he pulled his car over and sat on the edge of the road. The fear that had clutched him all day didn't come close to the fear he felt as he looked at the clock on his dashboard and saw the time and the date: it dawned on him they were at the halfway mark before Layla returned to her family.

He sat there for a long time, because it took a very long time for him to process it. He had never known love nor loved anyone before.

He had cared for others—sometimes a little, sometimes a lot—but he had never actually known love, and now here it was.

He didn't want to get closer to her—there was no point, because very soon she would be gone.

When she called he didn't pounce; he did not want to feel the way he did. But he answered his phone on the third ring.

'I know it is wrong to call you so late...'

Layla gulped and he closed his eyes, for he did not want to be moved by her distress, and yet his heart twisted as she continued.

'But it is an emergency of my heart, Mikael. I can't stop crying.'

CHAPTER ELEVEN

SUNRISE FOUND MIKAEL back in her bed, but wearing only hipsters this time, with Layla asleep by his side. He inhaled the traces of bergamot in her hair—it was fading.

Nothing had happened last night. Layla had been crying too much and it had taken for ever for her to go to sleep.

He didn't love her, Mikael decided in the warm light of morning. Instead, he told himself, it was as Layla herself had once said—he was attracted to her, perhaps a bit infatuated.

His world operated much more easily when it was devoid of love.

He picked up the snowglobe she had given him as she stirred awake beside him and watched snow fall for the first time on the Opera House.

'It doesn't snow in Sydney,' he said. 'Not since 1836.'

'It's a global warming snowglobe,' Layla said, curling into him, loving the feel of her leg sliding over his. 'The weather is doing crazy things everywhere.'

He stared at the settling snowflakes, wishing that she did not make him smile so easily.

If he did love her, then it was a very pointless love.

'What time are we leaving?' she asked, and Mikael's jaw gritted—because just to stop her crying he had suggested that today she check out of the hotel and they go to his home.

He'd rather hoped she might have forgotten his offer. Mikael's home was his haven. He had needed to be there the other night just to get away from the case, and he did not like sharing it with anybody else.

It was either here or to his city apartment that he brought women.

'I was just thinking about that,' he said. 'It's probably not such a good idea. There are no clubs or anything—just beach.' He'd hoped that Layla would decline, yet she seemed delighted with the idea.

'I would love to go to your home,' she said. 'And even if there aren't any nightclubs there shall still be dancing,' She smiled. 'Thank you!'

She felt calmer this morning. Last night had been horrible. After Mikael had stormed off she had realised just how selfish she had been—not just to Mikael. She was glad he was putting her brother's mind at ease but so terribly worried too, because Zahid would demand to know why Mikael had been with her at those times.

He would sort all that out, Mikael had said.

She hadn't believed him last night, but this morning she did. Because, warm and safe in his arms, she was sure that there was nothing he could not do.

'Before I take you to my home I have to go and see Demyan,' Mikael said. 'His wife has just had a baby and I need to visit. While I am gone you can sort out your stuff, and then I will come back and you can check out.'

'What present are you taking for the baby?'

'A snowglobe?'

'Mikael!' Layla scolded. 'That was my present to you. You have to keep it for ever. Though you *do* have to take a present for the baby,' she said. 'We can go shopping and choose one, and then I would love to meet your friends. We can go on the way to your house.'

He said nothing, but Layla was becoming literally too close to home for him.

Checking her out proved just as complex as checking her in.

A case was needed for the rather remarkable amount she had accumulated, and even the chef came to say farewell to her. Terrence carried the flowers that Mikael had bought her.

It was only as they drove off that it dawned on Layla that she wouldn't ever stay there again, and as they passed the court she struggled to come to terms with the fact that the magical day she had spent watching Mikael was the only one she would ever have.

She had planned her getting here so hard, and had been so determined to have fun and to cram all she could into her one special week, but it had never occurred to her that it might kill her to say goodbye.

And that was just to the hotel staff.

It was starting to dawn just how hard it was going to be to say goodbye to the other.

For both of them.

They stopped at the very boutique Layla had escaped from and bought a cashmere blanket and some little clothes and waited as they were gift-wrapped. Then they stopped at another boutique and bought a bikini and some beach dresses for Layla, before heading to Demyan and Alina's very luxurious penthouse.

'What is Demyan like?' Layla asked as they took the elevator up.

Mikael just shrugged, not quite comfortable with the cosiness of it all.

'Surely he's not as talkative as you?' she teased. 'What about his wife?'

'I have only met her a couple of times,' Mikael

said. 'She seems more pleasant than the first wife, but the bar was not set very high.'

Back to cynical, Mikael told himself. It was safer that way.

'This is Layla,' Mikael introduced her.

Alina was sitting down, holding the baby, and Demyan looked as if he hadn't shaved or slept since they'd last spoken. Mikael tried to ignore the slight start of surprise on Demyan's face. He had never brought a woman to his friend's home before.

'Actually, this is Princess Layla, and she's on the run.'

'You said not to tell anyone,' Layla scolded. 'You said that I was not to use my title.'

'Demyan and Alina are fine,' Mikael said. 'Congratulations!' He gave Alina a brief kiss on the cheek and then peered at the baby. 'She's beautiful,' he duly said.

'It's okay, Mikael.' Alina smiled. 'I'm not going to breastfeed in front of you.'

Mikael actually smiled at someone who wasn't Layla. 'Okay, I will have a seat, then!'

Despite his reluctance to bring her along with him, Layla made the whole visit so much easier for Mikael. She handed over their gift to Alina and oohed and ahhed over the baby while Mikael and Demyan walked over to the bar, where they chatted for a while as they shared a congratulatory drink, speaking in Russian.

'She's gorgeous!' Demyan said. 'You are good together.'

'We are good together because she's temporary,' Mikael said.

'So was Alina,' Demyan said, and they shared a wry smile because Alina had started as Demyan's temp.

'Well, in this instance it really is temporary. Layla has to return to her family in a few days.' Mikael shrugged as if it really didn't matter. 'I'll probably be bored with her dramas by then.'

He very much hoped that he would be.

But he doubted it very much too.

'How is fatherhood second time around?' Mikael asked.

'Just as good,' Demyan said. 'Actually, better. I

know a bit more what I am doing than I did with Roman. Alina is a natural mother.'

Even though they spoke in Russian this was all a foreign language to Mikael. What was a 'natural mother'? He looked over to his friend—a man he had had a fist fight with a few months back, when Mikael had suggested that he stop paying child support for his son, given that Demyan's ex-wife had told him that Roman might not be his.

Mikael had laughed then at Demyan's passion.

He was starting to glimpse it now.

'Why does she have to go back to her family?' Demyan asked.

'Because they love her,' Mikael answered, 'and because she loves them too.'

'Mikael—?' Demyan started, but Mikael shook his head.

'Don't.'

There was no point discussing it, for there was nothing he could do.

As they headed out to the elevator Layla was all smiles, but when the doors closed she rolled her eyes.

'What does that mean?' Mikael asked.

'You know.' Layla smiled.

'No.'

'All my cousins have babies, and you hold them and you smile, and you say the right thing, but...' Layla held out her palms in a helpless gesture. 'Then you run out of things to say.'

Very reluctantly Mikael smiled, but that was enough incentive for Layla to speak on.

'Now Trinity and Zahid are having a baby it will be the same with them. That was how I escaped. Trinity was watching me like a hawk, but I suggested we go in a baby boutique and once we were in I might just as well have not been there.'

'You don't like babies?'

'I don't *dis*like them,' she said, 'though they do freak me out a bit, with their big heads and eyes. I know I shall love mine, but really I would love more of this.'

'Of what?'

'Kissing and dancing,' she said as they stepped out of the elevator. 'Anyway, pregnancy isn't always a good thing...'

'Are you worried that it might ruin your figure?' He smiled.

Just when he thought he knew a little of what went on in her mind, Mikael found out there was so much more he didn't know.

'No.' Layla shook her head as they stepped out onto the street. 'I worry about death, given that it was pregnancy that killed my mother—she died giving birth to me.'

'Layla...' He went to catch her wrist but she shook it off.

'It is not something I wish to speak about,' she said.

'You can.'

'What's the point in that?' she challenged.

There was none.

They walked to the car in silence.

Layla was dreading a future with Hussain by her side.

Mikael felt suddenly ill at the thought of the same.

It was a bit strained on the drive to his property. Layla was lost in her thoughts and Mikael glanced over several times, trying to work out what she was thinking. Layla wished she hadn't told him that, for she did not like to discuss her fears about getting pregnant, and there was nothing that could be done about them anyway.

So, as they left the city behind, rather than sit in pensive silence Layla nagged him to teach her to drive instead.

'Please, Mikael....' she said, for perhaps the twentieth time. They were miles from anywhere and there was barely a car on the road, just mile after mile of ocean, and then a low white property came into view and she glimpsed what must be his luxurious house. 'Please let me drive.'

'No,' Mikael said as they pulled up on his huge drive.

He took her case in and left it in the hall as Layla looked around.

It was like nothing she had ever seen—a green oasis, and the tropical bush land outside seemed a feature of the home.

The place gleamed with a mixture of modern appliances and a few treasured antiques. A huge black and silver globe hung in one corner, and Layla guessed rightly that it was perfectly angled.

'I am there,' she said, pointing straight to Ishla.

If only the world were really that small, Mikael thought as she clipped on high heels through his home.

It was terribly hard for him to comprehend that the last time he had been home Layla hadn't existed in his world.

'Oooh, I like your chess set.'

'Leave it,' he said, watching her fingers hover over his knight. It felt strange having her here—a streak of feminine beauty in a home that was very male. He did not like the way her eyes seemed to take in each ornament, or each book that lined the walls, and he tried to distract her with the delicious view.

As they walked through to the lounge there was a stunning view of the Pacific Ocean, with its waves constantly rolling in, and Mikael opened the French windows to let in the magical sound .

'Do you want to go the beach?' he offered.

'Maybe later.' She shrugged and with a complete lack of boundaries walked through the house to his bedroom, which looked out onto the water also.

'Where are the maids?' Layla asked with mild interest.

'I don't have maids,' Mikael said. 'I have someone who comes in daily when I am here and weekly at other times.'

'So it really is just us?'

He should be offended, Mikael thought as she snooped through his wardrobe and then into his study, except he couldn't be, for she simply had no concept of living alone.

She thought his home was very beautiful and absolutely intriguing. Unlike the palace, Mikael's walls were not lined with portraits of ancestors, for he did not know from where he came. Instead the art was modern, and Layla stared at a red line on the wall that was fractured in several places before continuing and branching out.

'What is that?' She frowned and peered closer.

'It's a lifeline,' he said, admiring his favourite piece. It had cost an absolute fortune and it spoke to him in many, many ways—not just about this past but about his clients, their victims.

'A lifeline?' she queried. 'Oh, you mean like this?' She held up her palm and then looked back at the painting and pointed to the first fracture. 'So is this you in Russia?'

'It's just a painting.'

It was more than that, though, to Mikael, and he looked at it and thought of the future and the next fracture that would appear when Layla left.

She wanted to know more—there was so much that she wanted to know—yet intuitively she knew that he had already shared more than he was comfortable with. It might take months, possibly years, to truly know him, and all they had were days.

'Layla...' Mikael broke the tense silence because there was a question that needed to be asked. If she felt a tenth of what he did then something needed to be addressed. 'Are you sure that you want...?'

She did not want his question—she did not want this tension that was building to a head—and so she interrupted him before he could say what he must not.

'I actually think I could paint that,' she said stepping back from the painting and nodding. 'If you got me some red paint I could do another one for you…' She turned and saw his rigid lips and kissed them. 'I'm playing,' she said. 'Well, sort of.' Because she was quite sure that she *could* paint it—after all it was just a broken red line! 'I love your home. It is very…' she tried to think of a word to use '…very Mikael.'

'So, what do you want to do?' he asked, because he didn't like her examining his things.

'I already told you—I want to learn to drive,' she said.

'Layla, it's not something you learn in a few days,' he explained. 'Wouldn't you prefer to be doing other things?'

She looked at his delicious mouth and then back to his eyes.

'Teach me to screw, instead.'

Deliberately he did not blink. Mikael knew she had picked up that word from him, and really he would prefer that she didn't return to Ishla with that in her vocabulary.

'That's not a great choice of word, Layla.'

'You said it the other night—you said that she didn't want to lose a good—'

'Lover,' he said, but that didn't work—because he had never been in love until now, and what was the point of falling in love when any day now she'd be gone?

'I want to come again,' Layla said.

'That's better.'

'I want you to come too. I want to see.'

Still he did not blink, but Mikael chose the safer option. 'I'll teach you to drive.'

He watched the smile play on her lips as they headed back out to his car. 'You think you won there, don't you?'

'I think I did.'

He turned the car around and went through a few basics with her, but she just kept turning his radio on. 'Listen to me, Layla' he said, turning the music off for the third time. 'If I say brake then you are to brake—there is to be no arguing.'

'I know.'

'I'm in charge here…' Mikael warned, but he saw the press of her lips and the dark mood that had been building since last night inched towards breaking point. Was she serious about anything? he wondered, though he had enough insight to know he wasn't talking about driving.

A mini-tornado with black hair and eyes had spun into his life and changed every part of it, and she didn't even seem aware of the damage she would leave behind.

'Layla!' he warned as her fingers moved towards the stereo, and the anger in his voice was more than was merited, perhaps, but it came from within.

'Can I just remind you that I am a princess…?'

He climbed out of the car with his mounting temper and walked back to his sprawling home. She rushed after him.

'Don't walk away from me,' Layla ordered. 'Mikael. You do *not* walk away from me.'

She soon changed her mind when he turned and

she saw the look in his eyes as he strode back towards her.

'Okay, you can go now,' she said, but he did not stop walking till he was right in her face.

'Never,' Mikael said, 'pull the princess rank on me.'

'But I *am* one.'

'Don't we all know it?'

'You're cross with me.'

'You—' Mikael was on the edge of losing his temper; he never did—nothing goaded him, *he* was the goader '—are the limit. Have the keys.' He tossed them at her. 'Better yet, I'll take you back to the hotel and leave you there. Better still, I'll take you back to the city and leave you on the street. I'm done.'

He bent down to pick up the keys from the ground and headed back to the car. It was better that he was away from her; she'd have his heart otherwise.

'Come on.'

'Where?'

'I just told you.'

'You can't leave me in the city.'

'I am,' he said.

'Everyone is looking for me.'

'You'll be very easy to find,' he said, and opened the door for her. 'In.'

'No.'

'In.'

'No.'

'Fine,' he said, 'then you get to stay at the house. I'm off to the hotel…'

He started the engine and she ran in front of the car.

He sat with the engine idling, in air-conditioned comfort, as Layla stood in the hot Australian sun, and he was a fool to even pretend that he did not love her.

Life, Mikael thought as she came round to his window, had been so much more straightforward without her in it.

She tapped on the window and waited as it slid down.

'Please don't go.' she pleaded, but he said nothing. 'I was playing and I should have listened.' Still Mikael stared ahead. 'I'm sorry,' she mumbled.

'For…?'

'Not listening when you were trying to teach me.'

He went to slide up the window.

'For being a princess.'

'You can be a princess, Layla, just not when it's the two of us. Do you get it?'

'I think so.'

Even *he* was having trouble defining it. 'When I say enough, or stop, or there is danger, you must listen to me without question.'

'You are just like my brother and father—'

'Please,' Mikael dismissed. 'Do you know, I'm actually starting to lean to their side? If they've had to put up with your dramas for the last twenty-four years I'm full of admiration, in fact, that they got you to adulthood alive.'

'We only have a couple of days and you spoil them by being mean to me,' she said.

'You forgot to stamp your foot.' He saw her

tense, frustrated face as still she did not get her way. 'It won't work with me, Layla.'

'It worked before.'

'It won't work in the important things. Now, do you want to learn to drive?'

'Yes.'

'Who's in charge when you're a learner driver in my car?'

'You are.'

She climbed in, and this time Layla did listen.

Half an hour later they bunny-hopped back into his long drive...

'More to the left,' he said, his hand hovering over the handbrake, and wondered if he should take the wheel. But she righted the car—though a fraction too late.

'What was that noise?' Layla asked.

'My paintwork.'

'Oh.' She pulled to a halt, actually quite smoothly. 'How did I do?'

'Very well,' Mikael said, wondering why he wasn't jumping out of his car to inspect the damage; instead he leant his head back on the headrest and gave up fighting it.

Pointless and hopeless, perhaps, but in love was where he was.

She was the important thing.

Which meant that something had to be discussed.

And this time when he raised it he wouldn't let Layla interrupt him.

CHAPTER TWELVE

THEY UNPACKED HER case and Layla put on her new bikini. They had a swim at the beach until, salty and dusty with sand, they returned home hungry.

Layla was determined to make lunch herself.

Hair tied up, her new bikini damp, she was frying a practice prawn in butter with Mikael behind her, telling her to turn it when it went pink.

'It looks beautiful,' she said. 'I can't wait to tell my father about them.'

'Do you want to go back to Ishla?' Mikael asked the question he had tried to before, when Layla had been looking at his painting.

'Of course I do.'

She didn't even hesitate in her response, but Mikael persisted, knowing her answer had been automatic.

'Are you sure that you do?' He saw her face turn just a little and her lovely smooth brow was marred by a frown.

Until this morning she had not considered that she might have to say goodbye to people she cared about. Until now it had never entered her head that she might not want to go back to Ishla.

That she had a choice.

'Of course I am sure,' Layla said, though her voice suddenly said otherwise. 'I love my family.'

'I know that you do.'

'It would kill my father if I left.' Her voice started to rise as she pointed out the reality. 'It would honestly *kill* him.'

'Okay,' he soothed.

'I don't like that question,' she said. 'I don't like how it makes me feel inside. Please don't ask me things like that again.'

'I won't.' Mikael turned off the gas and, still behind her, wrapped his arms around her and held her till she relaxed back into him. But he could feel that her heart was racing—as, he guessed, was her mind.

'Go,' she said, because his words had unsettled her. 'Go and have your shower. I want to make lunch by myself.'

Mikael left her to it, mentally kicking himself and wondering if he could have handled that any better.

What the hell had he been thinking?

Suppose she'd said no, that she *didn't* want to go back?

What then?

Had he been asking her to be his *wife*?

Layla was determined to make a beautiful lunch—and she would if the butter knife she was trying to cut a tomato with didn't flatten it so.

And the onion had made her cry.

Or was she just crying?

Damn you, Mikael, for asking me that, she thought. *Damn you for making me stand here and cry and not want to go home to the land and the people I love.*

'Mikael!' She was suddenly angry and walked through to the bedroom. She could hear the shower was on but had no qualms about walking in. After all, he had bathed her a few times.

What Layla saw, though, had her heart in her throat—and suddenly she wasn't angry any more.

He looked up and saw the shock on her face as his eyes lifted from where he had been concentrating and he saw her standing there, watching him.

Then he watched her as the shock changed to a delicious smile and she stepped into the shower with him.

'Continue,' she said.

Mikael wasn't sure that he could—until her mouth started working his chest.

'Is this why you have so many showers...?' she asked, and he gave a half laugh. 'I thought you were just very clean!'

She loved the tension in him, loved the feel of his wet skin, and she slipped out of her bikini and then boldly dropped to her knees and kissed up his legs...slow kisses that changed to frantic, because she wanted so badly to touch and to taste what she must not.

He almost pulled her up by her hair, but he wanted her to see this, and wanted her pleasure too. He took her hand and placed it over his, on the outside, so that she did not touch, but she felt the motion and the building tension.

'Oh...' It was the nicest thing she had ever felt.

He bent his knees a little and rubbed himself over her and Layla watched in fascination, till her thighs were shaking.

'Mikael...' Every stroke brought her closer, and then she watched as their hands stilled but his shaft didn't, and the moan that came from him as he shot over her was addictive, for she wanted to hear it again and again. It was that and the shots of silver that spilled over her that almost brought Layla to her knees with her own lovely orgasm.

'What's that noise?' Layla gasped, at the sound of bleeping, but she was talking to thin air as Mikael had suddenly bolted from the shower. 'What is happening?' she asked, following him out. 'Mikael, what is that smell?'

Layla found out what a fire extinguisher was

as a naked Mikael tackled the wok that she had left unattended.

'You're supposed to turn the gas off,' he said as he put the small fire out.

'You shouldn't have turned me on.'

She had an answer for everything, and Mikael stood back breathless and looked at the smoke on his gleaming walls. All he could think was that he was going to miss this.

'*I'll* make lunch,' he said. 'First, though, I'm going to get dressed…'

'Why?' she asked, wrapping her arms around him. 'I like us like this.'

So too did Mikael.

'Do you want to watch some pawn while we eat?'

He gestured to the chessboard and Layla nodded.

'You didn't laugh at my joke,' he said.

'I don't joke about chess,' she said.

But he realised she probably had not understood.

They had a very quick and less ambitious lunch, which consisted of tomato sandwiches with loads of black pepper, and then, naked, she took two chess pieces, shook them behind her back and held out her hands.

Mikael peeled open the fingers on her right hand. He was black. There was a thrill of anticipation for Layla as he set the board up, and she lay on her stomach, propped up on her elbows. She had had the same flurry of nerves in her stomach when she had first played with a stranger online.

A better flurry, in fact!

'I don't want any favours,' she warned.

'You won't get them from me.'

Layla was white, within three moves it was Mikael attacking and Layla on the defence.

He watched as she removed his knight and then he swooped.

'*Mchfesa*,' she said.

Mikael could guess what that meant.

He set up again, and she opened as she had before, but again it was to no avail.

'I am *good* at this!' she said.

'You are.' Mikael smiled. 'But I'm better.' He wasn't pulling rank. 'I've played a lot.' And, as naturally as breathing, he told her a bit about his time on the streets and how chess had saved his sanity.

He didn't want pity, and he didn't get it from Layla.

'I have played a lot too,' she said. 'I would be out of my mind otherwise. Before I had my students, chess was the best company I had.'

Mikael looked up. 'Have you ever heard the saying, "at the end of the day the pawn and the king go back in the same box"?'

'No.'

She thought about it for a moment too long.

'Checkmate.' He smiled. 'You are too easily distracted. You need focus.'

'I will beat you one day,' she warned, and then he saw her jaw clamp down, because no matter how they hid from the world and got lost in their own they were constantly reminded that the clock was counting down on them.

But instead of dwelling on that Layla focused on the game. She opened differently and awaited his response.

'I'm thirsty, Mikael.'

'Then get a drink.'

She didn't. She moved into attack again and again, and suddenly they were game on.

'I'm *very* thirsty, Mikael.'

'Good,' he said, refusing to allow her to distract him. 'Shall I get up and run a tap?'

She shot him a look and stood up. Usually nothing distracted Mikael, yet as she returned and repositioned herself a very ripe nipple might have done. Had he had his time again he would not have made the move that he did. Not that his face told her that, and he hoped she wouldn't see the opening he had given her, but as he watched her fork him with her knight he realised she had.

'Your phone is ringing,' Layla pointed out as she sacrificed her queen.

'So?'

He let it go to voicemail as they played on, and soon her pawn had crossed the board and Layla had reclaimed her queen.

She smiled at him, but it wasn't returned for his phone was ringing again.

'What the hell does Demyan want?' Mikael's voice was irritated.

'How do you know it is Demyan?' she asked as he stood.

'He has his own ringtone.'

'That's sweet!' she said, and watched as he took the call.

The vague irritation in his expression disappeared and his face snapped to impassivity. She had a growing sense of unease as Mikael spoke in length to Demyan in Russian.

'What did he want?' she asked when he ended the call, and when he did not answer her straight away she knew that something was wrong. 'Is it the baby?'

'The baby's fine,' Mikael said.

But just as she relaxed he took her hands, and she knew she was going to hear bad news.

'Layla, Demyan and Alina were so curious about you that they looked you up. Your disappearance has just hit the press. The police are looking for you...'

'No…' she whimpered. 'No.' She shook her head. 'They won't find me here.'

'Yes, Layla, they will,' he said. 'The staff at the hotel will recognise you, and the booking was under my name. This is serious now.'

He let go of her hands, turned on the television and found the news.

There she was: black eyes, black hair, and a face that was unforgettable.

The police could be there in a matter of moments.

'We need to get you back.'

When she didn't respond he elaborated.

'Layla, it will be better for you if you return under your own steam than have the police find you.'

'One more night,' Layla begged. 'Mikael, please, I just want one more night.'

She was not manipulating him now; instead she was pleading.

'Just one more night and then I promise that I will go back happy. I will never interrupt your life again, Mikael, if you will please just give me one more night.'

'One more night...' he said. 'We'll take out my yacht...'

He was already loading a cool bag with supplies: champagne, fine food—anything he could think of to give Layla the very best final night.

'Go and get dressed and sort out the clothes that you'll return to your family in.'

'Mikael?' She frowned. 'I'll get changed here, tomorrow, after our night.'

'We won't be coming back here, Layla. If we're going to leave then it has to be now.'

It was the most horrible thing she had ever heard, and she simply did not now how to respond.

'Layla?' He was very calm; he could see how much she was struggling. 'Come on,' he said, deciding to find clothes for her. Just now it had nothing to do with her being a princess that she could not dress herself.

She was simply trying not to break down.

They were heading to his car in a matter of moments.

'Mikael…?' She said as he opened the passenger door for her.

'You're not driving.'

'No, of course not.' She was suddenly serious. 'Tonight, if I tell you to make love to me, if I plead with you that I don't care, please…'

'You'll be fine, Layla.'

She would be—he knew that.

But only for as long as she was in his care.

CHAPTER THIRTEEN

IT FELT LIKE the last night on earth.

Mikael sailed the yacht till it was far enough from his home that he was satisfied they would not easily be found, and then dropped anchor in a pretty cove.

He looked over to where she stood, leaning on the rail and looking out to the view, and he wondered how he could possibly give her the night of her dreams while knowing that tomorrow she'd be gone.

She could feel his eyes on her as she looked out at the view, at the gorgeous red sky. The next sunset she saw would no doubt be on her way back to Ishla.

Why had Zahid let her father know?

Tears stung her eyes because she had not wanted to hurt her father.

She remembered her threats to Zahid and Trinity that she would go to an embassy—she would never have done that, though. All she had wanted was a week.

'It is beautiful,' she said as Mikael came and joined her. But not even a sunset could soothe the hurt. Instead it made her want to cry. 'Why did they have to tell my father? Why did the police have to get involved?'

'I would guess they were very worried last night, when I didn't text and say that you were okay until so late.'

'I should have called and let you know that I was safe,' Layla admitted. 'It truly never entered my head. If I had had a phone there were a few times I would have liked to call you to tell you what was happening, but I don't have one.'

'I know,' he said, and put his arm around her shoulders. He looked out to the night and wished he could take away their row.

It had been no one's fault—she didn't know about public phones and, after all, he had told her not to ring him unless it was an emergency.

For Mikael, not wanting his day to be interrupted by her felt like a very long time ago.

'You were right to text Zahid, though,' she said. 'I was thinking about it after you left me alone last night. I believe that had you not texted him the first night to say that I was safe then my father would have been informed by the morning. At least we had *some* time.'

'You didn't get a week,' Mikael said, 'but have you had a nice few days?'

'They have been wonderful,' she said. 'You have been wonderful to me.'

Mikael made her favourite dinner—*without* setting the kitchen on fire—and she sat on the bench and watched him.

'Sick of prawns yet?' he asked.

'Never.'

They took their dinner up on deck and washed it down with champagne, and Layla shivered a bit when he asked her what would happen when she went back to Ishla.

'I know you said there would be trouble for you, but can I ask what sort?'

'I expect that my father will ban my computer,' Layla said, 'and I will have to apologise to Trinity and Zahid, and perhaps I will not be allowed to teach...' She ran a hand through her hair and thought of the smiling faces of her students and how much they would miss her. 'I was selfish, I suppose. They will miss out because of me...'

'It might not be for long,' Mikael offered, but she shook her head.

'My father has already told me that my future husband might find it offensive if I work...I expect that decision will be made for him.' She told Mikael the truth then. 'My father will bring my wedding forward, I expect. I have been trying to avoid it, but he will say I have given him no choice.'

'Layla...'

'Please don't ask that question again.'

He let out a tense breath in exasperation, but she had not finished speaking yet.

'I am so loved and so happy at home,' she said. 'I wanted adventure—just one big adventure—

and I have had that, I just forgot the first rule of chess.'

'Tell me.'

'To look to more than the next move,' she said. 'I planned and researched escaping, being here, and all the things I wanted to do, but I forgot to consider the leaving part. I never thought it would hurt—it never even entered my head that I might prefer to live life here.' As Mikael went to speak she shook her head. 'I would never do that to my father, to my country, to my people.'

'Even if you won't be happy?'

'Of course I will be happy. I will just miss things here,' she said, and tried to hold back on just how much she would miss Mikael. It would not be fair to either of them.

She had not lied to him that first day. Revealing her thoughts always got her into trouble, and possibly never more so than now. It was imperative that she did not break down and tell him just how she was feeling.

'I wanted tonight to be wonderful,' she said, 'but all I feel like doing is crying.'

'Come here,' Mikael said and led her to the day bed where they lay for a lovely while.

'Do you have any regrets?' Mikael asked and she shook her head.

'You?'

'None,' Mikael said and then thought for a moment. 'I wish that I'd got you that joint.'

'I don't need it now,' Layla said because lying here next to Mikael with the stars shining so brightly and the feel of being in his arms she had her high. It was a gorgeous navy sky, so dark except for the stars and just the tiniest sliver of moon.

'That's the first thing I thought of when I saw you,' Mikael said, gazing up at the moon and remembering walking into his office and seeing her standing there in her silver dress. 'Make a wish on the new moon,' he said.

Perhaps he should not have said that, because he had just managed to get her to smile.

'I just made it,' Layla said, and turned her head and looked at him.

'You can't tell me what your wish is,' he warned.

'Okay.'

She looked up at him and thought how lucky she was to be here even if just for a little while. 'I've done everything,' Layla said. 'I have danced...'

'You can *really* dance!' He nodded approvingly.

'I have had a romantic dinner with a very romantic man. We have held hands, touched knees, kissed...' she looked over at him. 'We have exceeded my list with orgasms.'

'Good.'

'I have had flowers, a whole day in bed...' She counted things off. 'A day out sightseeing.'

'What was your best bit?'

'Apart from the orgasms? Then your verdict party,' she answered immediately. 'Have *you* enjoyed it, Mikael?'

'Very much?'

'What was *your* best part?'

He paused as he tried to think, but he could not choose a best part, from her biting her teeth at him on the day they met, taking out that ruby—there was not one part that he could list above another.

'It's all been good,' he settled for saying. 'Though I do feel bad about our row.'

'Mikael!' she scolded. 'I *loved* our row. If it wasn't for our row you wouldn't have had to calm me down and agree to bring me to your home...'

Mikael actually laughed. 'Were you manipulating me *then*?' He was impressed rather than annoyed. 'Do you ever stop?'

'Never.' She grinned. 'Every word I say is with the intent to get what I want...' She looked over to Mikael, still smiling and looking a whole lot happier than he had on the day they'd first met. 'Can we have sex like the actors do?'

That was the wish she had made.

And he would make it come true.

'Yes,' he said, and decided that for however long they had left he would simply let himself love her.

'You could film it with your phone and then we could watch it together afterwards,' Layla said as he led her down to the cabin.

'No!'

'It would be fun.'

'Not a chance,' Mikael said, and he meant it even though he was laughing.

He would miss her so.

'You are so good to me,' she said as she sat on the edge of the bath and watched him shave just so that he wouldn't mark her.

'Why wouldn't I be good to you, Layla?'

'All the people who think you are a savage bastard...' she said. 'They don't know you.'

'I don't want them to,' Mikael said.

He'd liked living under his lonely rock—a career that consumed nearly all of him and pretty meaningless sex had been enough till now. But tonight, for one last night, he stepped out into the sun.

'You remember what I said back at the car?' she said as he dried his face. 'That even if I beg...?'

'Layla, you don't have to worry about that,' he said. 'Right—where do you want me?'

'Sorry?'

'Am I coming home from work, or are we already in bed? What was happening in the episode of that TV programme you saw?'

She started laughing—on a night she'd thought she never would. It was a side to Mikael she had never seen.

They were drunk on lust and enjoying it.

'We're on a boat and sailing for ever,' Layla said as he took her face in his hands. 'Tomorrow never comes.'

They had shared many, many kisses, but she had never tasted him so tender as his hand traced her spine and then unhooked her bra. She felt her breasts naked against his skin; it made her ache from the inside.

It was Layla who went for his belt but then changed her mind. Her hand held him through the fabric, growing him, holding him, stroking him, till Mikael pushed her hand away and led her to the bed.

Layla lay there, watching him undress, and she slid under the sheet as a naked Mikael joined her.

He kissed not her mouth but the breasts he had never tasted, and Layla relished the gentle licks and soft sucks, looking down at his lips as he blew her nipple to a painful peak and then kissed down her stomach and then back upwards.

'Take them off,' she said as his fingers stroked her through her bikini bottom; she wanted to feel him there.

But Mikael would not.

And so she did.

She undid the sides as he kissed her, and they wrestled just a little with each other, and with self-control—and then Layla's hand went where it must not, and she held him with no barrier this time.

Mikael rose to his knees and Layla looked at him.

'Just a little way?'

'Not a chance,' he said, and his hand was over hers this time as she stroked him, feeling the soft, soft skin that encased his manhood, moving him closer to where she wanted him. And it was cruel, for they deserved more.

Mikael moved down the bed and kissed along her thighs, over and over, till she pleaded with him to taste her *there* again.

This time he pulled her legs so that they lay over his shoulders and down his back, and she felt every breath from him; the flicks of his tongue were intense and they made her sob with both need and frustration, for she wanted him inside.

He struggled to stay gentle, not to bury his face in her mound and suckle and nip and probe her till she was ready—for that was where his mind was, and so too was Layla's.

'I don't care, Mikael...' she said as her fingers tried to pull his head from her, as she tried to move her legs so he would slide up the bed and take her. 'I don't care what happens when I get back...'

But his arms held her legs down, and his tongue was more rapid and probing, and he took her from the edge of potential disaster to temporary oblivion. Yet even as she came to his mouth, even as her body rode the high, somehow it was not enough.

She still wanted more.

'I want to taste you,' she said, and she smiled as she felt him moan with want between her legs.

'You said...'

'I can do this,' she said—for she would make her own rules. She would never do it with another... she would marry Mikael the only way she could: with her mouth. 'Please, Mikael, I will only ever do this with you.'

He lay on his back and Layla lay astride him, lowering her head to the base of him and slowly kissing the long way up.

'My hair...'

She lifted it and tied it into a knot.

'That is better,' Layla said. 'Now I can concentrate.'

She kissed him with her eyes open—not just his lovely shaft but down to his balls, which she took one by one into her mouth and sucked gently, because every bit of this she wanted to remember for ever.

He tasted clean, and she was about to give thanks for all the showers he took, but the moan from him and the slight pressure on her head told Layla he might not appreciate a break for conversation.

She was as turned on as she had been when his

mouth had been on her, and she felt one hand cupping her bottom as his other hand guided her just a little further down.

She ran her tongue around the top and then swallowed him a little way down, and then more, over and over, working him with her hand, somehow imagining that the hips that bucked in her mouth bucked between her legs.

Yes, she married him—for she would never be as intimate with another, would never moan and purr in pure pleasure.

She forgot her stride for a second, coming herself as he moved in her mouth, and just as it subsided Layla got the shock of her life as he swelled and started thrusting and she felt the first splash of Mikael.

He had meant to warn her. Instead he'd been taken back at the speed and strength of his orgasm.

He heard a small gasp from Layla—and even in the throes of his pleasure she made him smile. Kneeling up, holding her mouth closed with her cheeks bulging, she was the only woman in the world who could be about to spit and somehow not offend.

But instead she took a deep breath and swallowed.

'Oh, Mikael!' She was truly stunned for a moment, but then she smiled. 'That was fantastic.'

'It was.'

'A little more practice and I think…' Her voice faded.

They had almost run out of time.

'Come here,' he said, and brought her back to his arms for their last night on earth together.

Neither wanted the morning.

CHAPTER FOURTEEN

MIKAEL DID NOT sleep.

All night he heard the buzzing of a helicopter and wondered if it was for them—or more likely an air search that had nothing to do with Layla.

As she started to stir he kissed her head and smelt her hair. It smelt of the ocean and their time had run out.

She woke but did not open her eyes, because she didn't want it to be today.

'Layla?' He turned. 'I know you're awake.' He watched her smile with her eyes closed and he smiled at her too. 'Do you want breakfast?'

'No, I feel too sick to eat.'

Her eyes were still closed and he saw just the tiniest glimmer of moisture at the edge of them. He did not want to make this harder for her, even if it was almost killing him.

'Thank you for giving me a lovely last night,' she said.

'It was my pleasure.'

She opened her eyes and knew she wanted to open her eyes to him every morning; it felt as if this was the way the world should be for ever, with Mikael on the pillow beside her.

His eyes roamed her face and he took her hand. He had never wanted love and yet here it was now—and he was about to lose it.

'Marry me?'

She heard the words and they made her chest hurt. They made her eyes sting and they made her heart soar—and yet it plummeted in the next instant at the absolute impossibility of any future for them, so she answered him in the way that must serve them best.

She laughed.

'Layla...' He would not be swayed. 'I will sort it with your family. I will speak with your brother...'

'Mikael, you would be bored without your cases.'

'I mean marry me and live *here*,' he said, and she sat up and hugged her knees to her chest.

'Mikael, I live in a palace. As beautiful as your home is, do you really think I would want to give up my life?'

He said nothing.

'Will you give up *your* life and live in Ishla?'

He took a breath. 'If you let me speak with your family we can work out exactly what we want.'

'You really think my father would entertain the idea?' Again Layla laughed. 'Of course not. And so it is time for me to return to my family. I told you that if you gave me one more night then I would return happy. Now I keep that promise to you.'

Mikael sat as she headed to the bathroom. There was no request for assistance this time; in fact she closed the door.

Layla stared at her reflection for a very long time, telling herself over and over that she could do this. Reminding herself that she was going back to a family whom she loved very much.

Except on the other side of the door was a man

she loved in a different way; he was there in her heart, and she felt right now as if that heart was breaking.

She pulled on her silver dress and slippers and felt as if she was dressing for her own execution.

Mikael!

She wanted to scream his name, to plead for him to sort this, to go to bed now and wake up in a year in his arms to find out that it was all somehow over.

Instead she pushed open the bathroom door.

'Can you take me back to my family now?' she said. 'I want my father to know that I am okay.'

Even the ocean was against them, for they slid through the water with rapid ease. Mikael wondered if there might be police waiting at his car—if their goodbye would take place right here—but as he approached, there his car was, as he had left it.

Layla looked at the silver car that had caught her eye before she had even met him, and as they approached Mikael examined the huge scrape down its side and tried to tell himself his more ordered life could return soon.

'I loved driving,' she said as he opened the door and she slipped into the passenger seat. 'I have done all the things on my list and more.'

She put on her own seatbelt, albeit a bit clumsily, but if he neared her she would bury herself in his arms and plead for him to keep her for ever.

Wendy called on Mikael's private number to say that the police had been in touch and had asked that he call them.

'Thank you.'

He did not relay the news to Layla, and neither did she ask what the call was about; instead they drove in near silence, but as the city approached she turned the radio on.

'Don't.'

Mikael went to turn it off but she stopped him.

'Let me hear.'

She was the headlines.

He heard her snort as the newsreader said that Princess Layla of Ishla suffered from seizures and might need urgent medical attention, but her mirth turned to a strangled sob as an interview with her father was played.

Even before the translation Mikael could hear grief and bewilderment in the old King's voice.

The translation even procured a sniff from Mikael—for, as cynical as he was, and as much as he wanted to be angry with the man, he could hear the love.

'I love my daughter; she is my most precious possession. Please, Layla, come back to your family. Please, whoever is hiding her, make sure she is safe. There is nothing for me if there is no Layla.'

Then there was a statement that said if there was no news by morning the King would travel to Australia to help in the search for his daughter.

It would be morning in Ishla in a few short hours, and at the sound of her father's promise Layla issued her instructions.

'Drop me near the hotel that Trinity and Zahid are staying at.'

'I'm not just dropping you off,' Mikael balked. 'I will come and speak with your brother.'

'No!' she shouted. 'No, you will not!'

'You really think I'm just going to let you out of the car and drive away…?'

'If you care about me that is exactly what you will do.'

It wasn't supposed to end like this, Layla thought, resting her head on the window. It was supposed to end happily; she was supposed to leave smiling.

She wanted to cry, wanted Mikael to turn the car around and drive her to his home, but she must never let him see that.

'Here!' she said as they passed the café where she and Mikael had once shared breakfast. She knew the way to their hotel from there. 'Drop me here.'

'I can't just—'

'It was fun,' she interrupted, her heart breaking. 'Can we please just keep it at that?'

'Layla—'

'Please,' she broke in, 'stop the car and let me out.'

It was the hardest thing she had ever done.

Followed by the hardest thing Mikael had ever done.

Watching her get out and simply leave.

* * *

He walked into chambers and didn't even have to tell Wendy not to speak. One shake of his head was all she got and he stepped into the cool dark of his office, trying to fathom that a few days ago he hadn't even known her.

The best thing that had ever happened in his life had gone and he had had no choice but to let her go.

He felt as if there had been a death.

Yet he'd never mourned like this before.

He was breathing hard, just trying to get used to the idea of fifty or so years on the same planet as Layla without ever seeing her, when his intercom buzzed.

He ignored it.

'Mikael?' Wendy knocked at his door.

'I don't want to hear it!' he shouted, and then turned as the door opened.

'Yes, you do,' Wendy said. 'The café where you have breakfast just called. Layla's there, apparently. They saw her on the news but instead of calling the police they have called you.'

'Tell them to take her out to the back!'

'They've tucked her away in a booth and put reserved signs on all the tables near her. Layla doesn't know that they've called you.'

Mikael ran.

He almost flew into the café, to see the smile of Joel.

'Layla's fine,' Joel said as he walked Mikael over. 'Well, she's crying. She came and asked if we had any coffees on sub. I don't think she really gets the concept, but she's so gorgeous who could say no to her?'

Not Joel—and certainly not Mikael.

Tears were streaming down her cheeks as she nursed her coffee and Mikael knew he was glimpsing the real Layla—the one who hid deep beneath the shining surface, the Layla he had been so privileged to get to know even just a little.

'Why are you crying in your coffee?' he said, and saw her jump a little.

And then she looked up and did not even try to wipe her tears.

'I'm very confused, Mikael,' she admitted. 'It

was supposed to be fun. I did everything I ever wanted and I don't understand why I feel so sad.'

Mikael moved into the seat opposite and took her hands without thought.

He looked at the little circular scar on her wrist and knew that even if it hurt them both he would try one more time—because not only did he not want her to go back, his guts folded over at the thought of her with another man, going through the trauma of having babies she simply wasn't ready for and might never be ready for.

He did not want her scared—and if she had to be then he did not want her scared in the world without *him*.

'Layla, I meant what I said this morning—will you marry me?' he asked again. 'I will sort it all out. I will speak with your brother, your father...'

'No.' She looked at him. 'It can never happen.'

'Layla—'

'Please, Mikael, you are making this worse for me. I just wanted to sit with my coffee and my thoughts before I face my brother. I am more scared than I thought I would be, and I am so cross with them for telling my father.'

Her tears ran silent now and he did not want her to leave. It was the last thing on earth he wanted, and yet he needed to do as she asked and somehow make this better for her, not worse.

Mikael knew he needed to make this about *her* now, rather than them.

'Is there anything I can do that will help?'

'There is.' She gulped. 'Will you speak with Zahid? Can you tell him that nothing happened between us...? Can you tell him that I stayed with your married friends and that you were not with me when you texted in the evenings and nights, that your friends let you know how I was...?'

'Will that make it easier on you?'

'Much,' Layla said. 'If my father thinks I was alone with a man...' She shook her head. 'He cannot know. But please only agree if you are sure you can act as though you have no feelings for me—as though I am the trouble you first thought I was.'

He moved into the seat beside her and she felt

his arms around her for the last time, then his mouth on hers. It was a very tender kiss, for Mikael had not shaved, but it was so loaded with passion it would burn her lips every time she remembered it.

'I don't know how to let you go,' he admitted.

'If you care for me you will. I love my family. They will be cross, yes, but you are not sending me to savages, Mikael—you are returning me to my family and to people who love me.'

He thought of her kitten-soft feet and how pampered and looked-after she had been, and of her father, who was devastated that she was missing and in agony that he might have lost her.

Mikael was in agony too.

'Please, Mikael—please don't make this worse for me than it already is.'

He couldn't say no to her, and so he said yes to the most impossible task of his life.

'We'll do it at my chambers.'

CHAPTER FIFTEEN

THEY WENT OVER and over their stories before Mikael would call Zahid.

'I'll have Wendy make up a bill for units of time.'

'Reduce them!' Layla gave a thin smile.

'Yep—and I'll add the hotel costs…'

'The hotel?'

'I'm sure they would have remembered you and called the police—your family will know by now that you stayed there, I'll tell Zahid that you stayed between there and Demyan and Alina's.'

He missed nothing.

Mikael called the hotel and asked them to send an amended bill—with the alcohol removed.

'Thank you.'

He even rang Demyan and Alina, just to firm up her alibi.

'*Every* night,' Mikael reiterated to Demyan in English, so that Layla heard it too, 'and you or Alina would call me and say that she was okay, and then I would text Zahid. The other night the baby was upset and crying and you simply forgot till much later to call me.'

'Okay,' Demyan said. 'Mikael, is there any way Layla can stay...?'

Mikael switched to Russian and Layla closed her eyes at his angry voice as he swore at his lifelong friend—because if there *was* any way Mikael would be utilising it now.

When he had ended the call Mikael switched back to being impassive, but Layla had glimpsed his anger and his pain and she knew he was hurting just as much as she was.

'Okay, Demyan and Alina know what to say if asked.'

'What if they mess up?'

'Forget that,' he said. 'They'll do the right thing by you.'

'You need to call my brother now.' Layla's voice was suddenly urgent. 'My father will be flying from Ishla if there is no news by morning. I want him to know as soon as possible that I am safe. He is ill…' She was starting to panic—not for herself but her father. 'Mikael, my father is sick and no one must know that. I should not have done this when he is so ill…'

'Calm down,' he said. 'I'll call Zahid now.'

'I have been trouble, remember?' she said as he punched in the numbers.

Zahid answered on the first ring. Mikael was certain he must have spent the last few days with his phone permanently to hand.

'Your sister has asked that you collect her,' Mikael told Zahid, and gave his address. 'She's fine,' he said. 'Yes, I put her in a hotel, but you were right—she's completely incapable and so I had a couple I know looking out for her.' His voice changed to irritated. 'They happen to have just had their first baby, so having your sister dumped on them was a huge inconvenience—'

Mikael pulled the phone from his ear. Zahid had hung up on him.

'How did he sound?'

'Relieved—which will soon turn to angry,' Mikael warned. 'But that's normal, and it will be the same for your father. It was the same for me when you didn't come back to the hotel that night.' He took her in his arms. 'Then, when they've calmed down, they'll remember how relieved they are because they love you. As do—'

'No.' She stopped him before he could say it. 'Those words belong between a husband and wife.'

He poured two glasses of sparkling water, added lime and ice and placed one either side of the desk as they took their seats.

'Have you any mints?' she asked, and he took a packet from his pocket and rolled them across the desk.

She didn't take one; instead she put them in her tunic—she would keep them for ever.

She wrote him a note and folded it. 'Read it when I am gone.'

'Is it in English?'

'No,' Layla said as he pocketed it, and tried with all she had to make their parting easy on him. 'It will be good to get back to my students.' She gave him a smile, for it was surely kinder to do that than to cry. 'And you can get back to your cases and your blonde girlfriends…..'

He said nothing—just looked at her for the very last time.

Sooner than they could ever be ready the intercom buzzed.

'They're here,' Wendy said.

Mikael knew he was tough, but he wasn't a patch on Layla. She put on her brightest smile and sat, her eyes rolling, as a furious Zahid marched in.

Then she stood and screamed at him in Arabic.

'English, please!' shouted a blonde woman—presumably Trinity. 'I want to know what the hell has been going on too!'

'I want to know why you called Father!' Layla shouted. 'All this could have been kept between us…'

'We didn't call your father,' Trinity said. 'Zahid said to leave it, to keep it between us. It was Jamila who couldn't…'

'How *dare* she step in?' Layla flared. 'How dare a lowly servant—?'

'That so-called *lowly* servant held you the day you were born.' Zahid was livid. 'That *lowly* servant loved you when your parents...' He halted.

Mikael noted it.

'Go and take your fury to Jamila, Layla. Go and shout at an old woman who has been weeping for days over you,' Zahid said. 'You are a spoiled brat and you always have been. Well, you got your way again—no matter the cost to everyone else. So, what have you been doing?'

'Having fun!' Layla shrugged. 'The same sort of fun you and Trinity have always had.'

'What sort of *fun*?' Zahid demanded.

'Expensive fun,' Mikael said.

'And you've paid for it for she had no money with her?' Zahid's eyes narrowed as he looked at Mikael. 'Why would you do that?'

'I had a retainer.' Mikael opened the safe and displayed the ruby. 'I'd prefer a wire transfer.'

The room was starting to calm down.

'Can I see your expenses?'

Mikael buzzed Wendy and asked her to bring in the current bill for Layla.

'Today hasn't been added yet,' Mikael said, and handed the paper to Zahid, who scrutinised it for a few moments. So too did Trinity, who frowned.

'How can you spend more than five hundred dollars on apples?' Trinity asked, but that was the least of Zahid's concerns.

'These friends of yours...?' He turned to Mikael. 'I wish to speak with them.'

'I doubt that they wish to speak with *you*,' Mikael responded coolly. 'Layla says that you two are expecting a baby of your own. Remind me to dump a problem like Layla in *your* lap a couple of days after your baby is born.'

'Zahid...' Trinity was the voice of reason. 'She's safe—that's all you need to know.'

Mikael watched as Zahid's jaw gritted and knew that Layla's brother was struggling to hold back tears of relief.

Layla was right: they loved her.

'We will go,' Zahid said, and glanced briefly

over to Mikael. 'Your account will be settled as soon as I return to Ishla. Or now, if you—'

'When you return to Ishla is fine.'

'Come,' Zahid said to Layla. 'We do not discuss our business in front of strangers.'

Mikael handed over the ruby and glanced at Layla, who looked defiant, angry, happy—a strange combination only she could manage.

She shot him a brief smile.

'Thank you for your assistance, Mikael.'

'You're welcome.'

That was it.

The coolest goodbye ever.

She turned and simply dismissed him, and Mikael stood there as they all walked out and did not flinch. He kept his face impassive.

For her sake.

Only when she was gone did he pull out her note and stare at the pretty curves and dots. He had no idea what she'd written.

Whatever it meant, Mikael felt it too.

For the first time in his life he did not have a solution.

For the first time in his life Mikael cried.

CHAPTER SIXTEEN

LAYLA RETURNED INTACT.

A little swollen, the doctor commented as she examined her.

'I know!' Layla said. 'There was no one there to bathe me! The hotel refused to send someone, and the baths are high there and not sunken. I slipped getting out. I am still very sore.'

She spoke with the same authority she always did and looked the doctor in the eye as she lied.

'Does my father have to know about that?'

The doctor hesitated, for perhaps King Fahid *should* know. Yet she was a kind woman, and she had been the one who had delivered Layla the awful day that her mother had died, and she had also fabricated the story about a seizure just to help Layla.

'Of course not.'

The King breathed out a long sigh of relief when it was reported that there was not a bruise nor a cut on his daughter's skin and that it appeared no harm had come to her. He sent for her and Layla stood, resigned, staring above and over his shoulder as her father delivered a very stern lecture and demanded more details as to what had happened in her time in Australia.

'You lied to me,' Fahid said. 'Even now you lie. What was the whole point of running away if all you were going to do was sit with people who have just had a baby? You don't even like babies.'

Layla breathed out through her nostrils.

'I want the truth, Layla,' her father demanded. 'Did you dance?'

'Yes, I danced,' she said.

'And drink alcohol?'

'Once.' She'd admit to once. 'I had an Irish coffee. I have wanted to try one since Zahid told me you could have whisky in coffee and the cream stays at the top.'

'What else?'

Layla said nothing.

'What else?' the King demanded. 'What else did you get up to?'

'I tried to get a joint.'

'A joint?'

'Weed,' Layla said. 'The same stuff that was found in Zahid's locker at school! I had always wanted to try it.'

'And did you?'

'No one would let me.'

'What about men?' the King demanded—for, like her mother, Layla had always dreamed of romance. 'Did you do anything of which you are ashamed?'

'No, Father.'

Her answer was the truth.

'Layla?'

'No, Father, I did nothing of which I am ashamed.'

'I'm *very* disappointed in you, Layla.'

'I know that you are.'

'Are you disappointed in yourself?'

'No.' She shook her head. 'I am proud of myself

and glad that I did it. I've had my rebellion. I am sorry that it had to hurt you.'

'You are supposed to say *yes*, you *are* disappointed in yourself.'

'But I'm not.'

'You won't be teaching,' he said, and saw her lip tremble. 'Who knows what you might suggest…?'

'I would never encourage poor behaviour in my students,' she said, 'but I *am* an adult—'

'Enough!'

The King went through her punishments.

'No more teaching…' He saw her chin jut. 'No phone.'

'I never had one in the first place.'

'No letters.'

Layla was relieved. Otherwise poor Mikael might need to get a wheelbarrow for the thousands of letters in Arabic that might be delivered to him—letters he could never understand. Her heart squeezed as she thought of the small note she had left him and wondered if he would ever work it out.

Perhaps it was better to have their contact severed so brutally.

'No internet—ever!' Fahid continued.

'What about chess?'

'You can play chess with me,' Fahid said. 'And next week you will select a husband.'

Layla said nothing.

'You don't argue?'

'I knew the consequences when I ran away,' she said. 'I knew what would happen when I got back.'

'And was it worth it?'

It was the only time the King had glimpsed a flash of tears.

'Yes.'

She was back, and plans had been made for Princess Layla to choose her husband tomorrow.

She was well, she was safe, she had returned.

The palace felt like a funeral parlour though.

The King looked out to the gardens below his study and saw Layla walking when usually she would have run.

She looked cold, even though the evening sun was still blazing before dipping below the horizon.

'How has she been?'

He turned when Jamila entered; he had asked to speak with her.

'She is very polite, she is doing everything that has been asked of her and she has given me no cheek—but she is very angry with me. I know that, even if she doesn't say so.' Jamila started to cry. 'I am sorry for interfering…you might never have known.'

'You were scared for her,' Fahid said. 'You were right to call me.'

He looked to the woman who had been like a mother to his child—Layla's only parent when he had not been able to be one.

'You were brave to go against Zahid and call me.'

He sat down, for he could not stand to look out of the window and see Layla so unhappy.

Fahid closed his eyes. He wanted this sorted. 'I have not got long…'

'Don't say that, Your Highness.'

'It is true, though. I just want to know she will be taken care of.'

He looked over, because again Jamila was crying.

'Jamila…?'

'I don't want you to die, Fahid.'

She was no longer speaking with the King but with the man who had come to her at night a year after his wife had died.

The man who had made love to her as Layla slept in her crib beside the bed.

The man who still came to her at times, even now.

Times that must never be discussed, for she was a servant—that was all.

Yet the King and Layla felt like Jamila's family, and she wanted more time with him—especially now.

'Perhaps the treatments will give me more time,' he said, and took his lover in his arms.

And if they did give him more time, Fahid thought, then perhaps he should use it wisely.

* * *

Fahid watched as Layla pushed her *hashwet-al-ruz* around her plate. It was her favourite—spicy rice with minced lamb and mint—and Jamila had told the kitchen to add extra roasted pistachios, which Layla loved.

Not tonight, though.

'You are not hungry,' the King observed.

'Not really.' Layla attempted a smile. 'Do we have prawns here?'

'Prawns?' The King frowned. 'You mean shrimp?'

Layla shrugged. She didn't know.

'We do, but I don't like it,' the King said, and waited for the smart answer that the old Layla would have given—something along the lines of, *So you don't like it and that means that I don't get to try it?* But instead she just carried on pushing her food around her plate.

'We could play chess tonight,' the King offered, but she shook her head.

'May I be excused?'

'Layla…' the King started, but then he halted. 'You may.'

'Am I allowed to go for another walk?'

'Of course,' he said. 'Enjoy.'

Abadan laa tansynii.

Mikael had managed to work out what the first part of her note meant and it had been painstaking. He could ask someone to translate it, but he wanted to do it himself and finally he had managed a little of it.

Don't ever forget me.

He never, ever could.

So much so that as Mikael read the brief for a new client he felt nauseous.

'He needs to find someone else,' Mikael said to Wendy.

He simply couldn't do it any more; he'd assuaged his guilt over Igor and now he was going to use his power for good.

What had Layla done to him?

He just had to know that she was okay.

He took out his phone and stared at it for a long time. He was worried that his calling might make things worse for Layla, but the payment of his fees had gone in today so there was almost a valid reason to call. He would keep his voice brusque, Mikael decided. He would thank Zahid for the payment and check that she was okay.

He just had to do *something*.

Layla walked through the palace gardens and had never felt more confused—because she had done more than she could ever have dreamed of in her few days away and so surely she should be happy. As she walked she remembered dancing and laughing with Mikael, and she remembered his kindness too. How he had come back for her that night and stopped her going out. How he had bathed her and watched over her.

She had laughed when he had asked her to marry him and yet it was the nicest thing that had ever happened to her. What she wanted more than anything in the world was to be his wife.

Yet it was impossible. For even if somehow—impossibly—her father agreed, imagine Mikael here, in Ishla…

She could not.

Oh, at first it would be bliss. But without his cases, without the life he had built from nothing, that bliss would surely fade. Layla could not do that to him; she could not bear to think of him living here, with his opinions invalidated by the King and later by Zahid.

No palace would be big enough for such strong men.

A sob came and she could no longer hold it in.

Her father might be watching her from the window, Layla knew, and she fled down a hidden path towards the second palace, where Trinity and Zahid lived. But she did not run to them. Instead she sat on a stone bench and wept and sobbed as she never had in her life—not even when she had gone to choose her suitor. This evening Layla cried not just for herself but for Mikael, for he had no family and yet it felt as if he was a part of hers, and she would never see him again.

'Layla!'

Trinity had been walking, and at first had thought an animal must be trapped, such was the distress she'd heard. Trinity put her arms around Layla's heaving shoulders and tried to find out what was wrong, but Layla shook her head at everything Trinity asked.

'Is your father still cross?'

Layla shook her head.

'Are you scared of choosing a husband?'

'No.' Layla gulped.

There was no room in her heart left to be scared.

'I fell in love.' Her tears calmed just a touch with the terrible admission. 'I always thought I wanted to fall in love but it is horrible…it is agony. Please, *please*, don't tell Zahid.'

'He might understand.'

'Even if he could understand it would make no difference, Zahid is not yet King.'

'Who?' Trinity asked. 'Who did you fall in love with?'

'Mikael.'

Trinity blew out a breath. Perhaps Layla was suffering from a serious case of a crush, because if Mikael loved her in return surely he would not have let her leave?

'I begged him not to let Zahid know there had been anything between us.'

'He's a brilliant actor, then,' Trinity said, remembering Mikael's bored expression.

'He did it for me,' Layla said. 'No one ever knows what he's thinking, yet he tells *me* how he feels.'

'He feels the same about you?' Trinity checked, and then double-checked again. 'You're sure that Mikael loves you?'

'He asked to marry me.'

'Mikael asked you *that*?'

'Yes.' Layla said. 'And I laughed because it is so impossible. I love my family. I did not know how to say yes to what I want without hurting all the people I care for. He tried to tell me that he loved me and I would not let him, because those words only belong in marriage. But I want to hear those words now, and I want to tell him I love him too. I wish I had at least said that. If I could speak with him just one more time...'

'Do you have his phone number?'

'No, he gave it to me but I tore it up.' Layla turned and managed a smile. 'I don't want his number—there would be too much temptation.' The tears had stopped but the sadness was still there and very possibly would never leave. 'I should get back to the palace.'

'Stay and talk,' Trinity said, but Layla shook her head.

'I had better not take too long...'

All the fight had gone out of her, Trinity thought sadly as Layla headed back.

Trinity walked into the second palace and looked at her husband. His back was to her as he gazed out to the ocean and his shoulders were set rigid. Trinity wondered if it would make things better or worse for Layla if she told Zahid.

She did not have to tell him, though—it would seem that he already knew.

'I think something went on with Layla and her

barrister.' Still Zahid did not turn. 'He has called to see how she is.'

'Perhaps it was just a follow-up call,' Trinity said, not sure how to tread here. She loved her husband so much, but some of the ways in Ishla she would never understand.

'I don't know if it was poor reception, but...' Zahid could not explain, and neither did he want to acknowledge the sudden husk in Mikael's voice near the end of his call. 'He asked to speak with her.'

'What did you say?'

'That it would not be wise. That she was happy to be back with her family.' Zahid turned then. 'She's not happy, though, is she?'

'No.'

'Has she spoken to you about what went on while she was away?'

'A little,' Trinity said. 'Zahid, please don't ask me to break her confidence.'

'I shan't.' He looked at the wife he cherished, despite once fearing love. 'Layla is very different to me,' he explained. 'She has always craved love. From the day she was born she screamed for it. She wanted to be held, to be cherished. Jamila did her best for her. I was seven when Layla was born, and I tried to be a comfort to her, but she wanted her mother. She wanted my father too, but she got neither...'

'Is there anything you can do to help her?' Trinity asked.

'I have tried.' Zahid sighed. 'You remember I had already agreed to choose a bride when we met again in London?'

Trinity nodded.

'The reason I had agreed to choose a bride was in order to postpone a wedding for Layla. I knew my father did not have much time. I wanted to change the rules for my sister.'

Zahid was conflicted too—angry with the man who had looked him in the eye as he'd lied to him.

'Have you seen the scum that Romanov defends?' Zahid sneered. 'I have looked him up and his reputation with women is—'

'I had a *terrible* reputation,' Trinity broke in. 'We both know that what people said about me was wrong.' She took a breath as she saw her husband waver. 'Layla herself says that they can never be together—she simply wants to speak with him one more time.'

Zahid did what he knew he should not: he handed Trinity his phone.

Trinity almost flew from the second palace. She chatted politely with the King for a few moments and then asked how Layla was.

'She is very...' The King halted. 'Layla has accepted all her punishments instead of fighting me.'

'Can I speak with her?'

'Of course—she is not a prisoner.'

Trinity smiled at Jamila, who opened the door of Layla's room as Trinity approached.

'I don't want to talk about it any more,' Layla said. She was lying on her stomach, reading the card Mikael had sent with the flowers. 'If I do I will cry, and I don't want to be sad when I think of him. I have this.' She handed Layla the card. 'This makes me smile.'

'Do you want me to read it to you?' Trinity offered.

'No, Mikael did, and I remember every word. *"Layla, thank you for an amazing end to a difficult day and an even more amazing night. Mikael."* And he gave me three kisses.'

Trinity smiled, but then frowned at the 'amazing night' part. 'I thought the doctor said…?'

'Trinity…' Layla would let her in on a very big secret! 'You don't have to have sex to have an orgasm—there are other things you can do.'

'I'll bear it in mind.' Trinity laughed—she just *loved* Layla.

She handed her Zahid's phone.

'You wanted to speak with him one more time,' Trinity said as Layla stared at it. 'Mikael just called Zahid to see how you were and asked if he could speak with you.' She put the phone down on the bed. 'I will go out on the balcony.'

Trinity couldn't hear the words, just the love and tears in Layla's voice as she tried to be brave and not break down, as she tried to sound upbeat for Mikael.

It was enough to make Trinity cry as she did her best not to listen to one side of their final conversation…

When his phone rang and he saw that it was Zahid Mikael answered it on the first ring—and then nearly folded when he heard Layla's voice.

'Mikael.'

'Layla.' *Thank God.* 'Are you okay?'

'Of course I am.'

'How was your father?'

'Disappointed, cross. I am to choose a husband tomorrow…and I cannot use my computer ever again. But I will work on that soon. Trinity has smuggled me Zahid's phone. This will be the last time we speak.'

'Don't say that.'

'It will be,' Layla said, and knew, for his sake, that she had to somehow keep this a little light— for even Mikael could not fix this. 'Our minds might meet now and then, but we won't speak or see each other again.'

Mikael frowned. Was she talking about dreams?

But Layla had changed the subject. 'How is work?'

'I don't want to talk about work. What do you mean, our minds will meet?'

'You will work it out,' Layla said. 'Now, I want to know about your work—how is it?'

'Nauseating,' Mikael admitted. 'I'm crossing to the other side.'

'Meaning?'

'Prosecuting the bastards.'

'Go you…' Layla smiled.

'How are your students?'

'I am banned from teaching at the moment. After the wedding perhaps I will get to teach again, but I don't think so.'

'Layla?' he asked, and she closed her eyes at the depth of his voice. 'Did I look after you?'

'Beautifully.'

'Is there anything you regret?' he said, for he worried that they might have gone too far.

'Just one thing,' Layla said. 'That I laughed when you proposed. Mikael, I laughed only at the impossibility, not the sentiment.'

'Can I *please* speak to your father?'

'You will not get a fair hearing.'

'I thought he was a fair man?'

'Not about this,' Layla said. 'There is something else I regret—that I did not let you say *I love you* and that I did not tell you that I love you, and that I shall for the rest of my life.'

Mikael felt his heart squeeze in pain, and then the knife in it twisted as she continued.

'I wish you had been my first. Then I could perhaps have been punished and made a spinster...'

'Layla...'

'I have to go. Jamila is knocking at the door. *Abadan laa tansynii,*' Layla said.

'I'll never forget you either,' Mikael replied.

'And I will love you for ever,' she said.

'I'll love you for ever too.'

Mikael's answer was honest. His response immediate.

He walked out and past Wendy and gave a shake of his head that said *not now.*

He went straight to his car and smiled at the

scratched paintwork before gunning it to the airport.

Layla loved him.

Which meant he was going to Ishla to plead his case.

CHAPTER SEVENTEEN

'RETURN OR ONE-WAY?'

'Return,' Mikael said, and then changed his mind, for he could not imagine returning without Layla by his side, and in dark superstition he said, 'One-way.'

'It's actually cheaper to buy—'

'False economy,' Mikael interrupted. 'I'm going to be fed to the dogs when I get there.' As he had with Alina, Mikael smiled again at another woman who was not Layla—for that was what Layla had done. She had been in his life for less than a week but, despite the pain of living apart from her, in ways he was happier than he had ever been for she made the world a nicer place.

'Enjoy!' The stewardess smiled back and handed the good-looking man his first-class one-way ticket to Ishla.

Mikael would not be enjoying the flight.

He would be working the hardest that he ever had in his life.

He asked for sparkling water with lime—their first drink.

And he asked for a peeled and finely sliced apple and raspberries.

He knew that he worked better hungry.

As he prepared for the biggest case of his life he had no distractions. He would focus purely on Layla, on every meal, every conversation they had ever had—and he did.

He went over and over it all in his mind, honing in on words, recalling with intricate detail every conversation that had been shared, and he worked out, too, who he might have in his defence.

Trinity was a given, Mikael immediately decided, for she had smuggled the phone.

Zahid?

He loved his wife and had caused controversy himself, given that Trinity had been pregnant when they'd got married, and with Trinity buzzing in his ear... Mikael asked for more water and recalled proud Prince Zahid close to tears when he had been reunited with Layla and knew that he loved his sister.

Yes, he had Zahid.

But it was Layla's father, the King, whose consent he required.

What did Mikael know?

He remembered Layla's eyes filling with tears, for her father was sick.

Noted.

It wasn't enough, though, Mikael knew. There was something he was missing—there just had to be more.

Jamila?

He thought of the old lady, who must surely love Layla, but she was set in her ways and would perhaps want tradition to be followed.

There *was* something missing, but Mikael did not know what. He was going into the biggest fight of his life and yet he felt unprepared.

Mikael pulled out his wallet and stared at the piece of paper she had given him and the dots and swirls that had proved so hard to decipher.

Intensely private, he did not like to ask for help, and he had done his best to work her words out for himself, quite content to spend the rest of his life learning Arabic if that was what it took. But now Mikael needed every detail.

When the stewardess came round to ask if he would like his bed prepared for sleep, Mikael shook his head and said that he would be working through the flight.

'Would you mind translating this note for me?'

'Of course.' She read it and smiled. '"Don't ever forget me",' she said. 'It is a love saying,' the stewardess explained. 'Then it reads, *"Wahashtini Malikah"*, which means *I miss you, Queen.*'

'Princess, perhaps?' Mikael checked.

'No.' The stewardess shook her head. 'That would be *Wahashtini Ameera.*'

It didn't make sense, but Mikael tried to work it out with the stewardess's help. 'Could it mean: I miss you, *from* your Queen?' Mikael frowned, for Layla had never said that in marrying Hussain she would one day be queen.

'No.' Again the stewardess shook her head. 'I

don't really understand what is being said—just that it reads, "I miss you Queen".'

It was then that he understood her words.

His heart was thumping in his chest as he took the small note back and stared at it with a smile.

Clever, *clever* Layla, he thought. So *that* was what she'd meant about their minds meeting at times...

It was her online chess name, Mikael was positive about that, but more than that—more than a future meeting of minds—he was starting to see that it was the Queen who was missing in his argument.

The Queen who, despite her absence, was still a huge presence in Layla's life.

A queen who had apparently been very similar to the daughter she had never met—a woman Layla herself had said would approve of her plans.

Mikael rested back in his seat and closed his eyes for a moment as his thoughts started to align.

If she *had* been like Layla it must have killed the King to lose her. Mikael was certain of that, for in the days since Layla had been gone, despite the joy she had brought, his heart had closed, his curtains had been drawn, and the world seemed a very dark place.

Mikael recalled Zahid's words in chambers when he had told Layla off about Jamila.

'That so-called *lowly* servant held you the day you were born. That *lowly* servant loved you when your parents…'

Zahid had halted.

Now Mikael was starting to understand Zahid's hesitation.

In his grief, had the King turned his back on his daughter?

Did Layla not even know that he had?

As the plane began its descent still Mikael continued working, examining every angle, refusing to let up as he prepared for the most important case of his life.

The plane was on its final approach, but Mikael saw not the desert or the ocean, nor the clusters of buildings and streets, but the huge palace that looked out to its people.

In there was Layla, preparing to choose the man with whom she would spend the rest of her life.

It had to be him.

He had to be right.

The plane landed and the passengers disembarked, and Mikael was searched at Customs and asked the reason for his visit to Ishla.

'I have heard it is a very beautiful land.'

'You have no luggage.'

'I want to wear robes,' Mikael said. 'I would like to blend in.'

A female customs officer was going through his wallet and pulled out Layla's note. She looked to Mikael. 'Do you know anyone in Ishla?'

'I have a friend who I play chess with,' he said, and told himself not to break out in a sweat. He told himself not to falter or blink or react as the officers chatted in Arabic and laughed for a moment.

'You are here for romance?'

'Hopefully,' he said, wondering if it was the right answer, if he would even get into the country, if this was the end of the line.

'Enjoy your stay in Ishla,' the female officer said, and handed the wallet back to him.

He arranged a hire car and then stepped out into the fierce sun. But before heading to the palace he rang Zahid. As expected it went straight to voicemail.

'I am in Ishla.' Mikael left a message. 'I suggest that next time you pick up.'

He gave it five minutes and then called Zahid again.

This time his call was answered.

'It is better that you stay away,' Zahid said, by way of introduction.

'I am not staying away,' Mikael said. 'I am here to speak with your father.'

'I cannot suggest strongly enough that you get on a plane and leave now.'

Zahid was speaking the truth. If his father found out that Layla had been in any sort of relationship while overseas then all hell could break loose—not just for Mikael, but for Layla.

'You need to leave Ishla.'

'That is not going to happen without my first speaking with your father,' Mikael said.

Zahid looked over to Trinity and then looked away.

'My sister chooses her husband this day.'

'Then I need to speak with your father before she does—and you shall arrange it.'

Zahid's jaw gritted. There were few who would speak to him like that, and his temper was starting to rise at Mikael's arrogance.

'It is not just my father you need to speak with.' Zahid's voice was black with anger. 'Layla is my sister and you will speak with *me* and explain yourself. How dare you lie to me and tell me she was nothing but an inconvenience? I want to know exactly what went on. I will send a car to collect you.'

'No need.' Mikael's smile was also black, for he did not trust Zahid not to have him driven out to the desert and left there. 'I'm in a car and on my way.'

He would shout to Layla from the palace gates if he had to.

Zahid ended the call and still he did not look at Trinity. Instead he called for Abdul.

'We have a visitor arriving shortly,' Zahid said. 'His name is Mikael Romanov and he is to be brought straight to the King's office, but he is not to be taken through the main entrance. You will tell my father to meet me there now.'

'Your father is entertaining Princess Layla's suitors and their families...'

'This is not a discussion,' Zahid said.

Now he spoke to Trinity. 'He wants to speak with my father. I will be there.'

'Can I be there too?'

'No.' Zahid shook his head.

'Why?'

'Because he does not need to convince *you*,' Zahid said. 'You have already made up your mind.'

'Zahid, please...'

'Trinity, you do not understand how delicate this is.'

'Your father has accepted me.'

'Layla is his *daughter*!' Zahid said. 'You came

and moved to Ishla—do you think Mikael will do the same? Do you think my father will let Layla leave the country?'

Trinity blinked as it dawned on her just how impossible this situation was.

'Never.' Zahid shook his head. 'My father will never agree to a commoner marrying his daughter, let alone taking her to live overseas. Go and help Layla get ready. You are not to let her know that Mikael is here.'

'Zahid, surely she should be able to see him? Even if nothing can come of it!'

'Trinity, I know my father and sister best, and I am asking you...'

'Or *telling* me?' Trinity challenged.

'Both,' Zahid said. 'You have to trust that I will try to do the right thing by my sister.'

Trinity did trust that Zahid would do his best.

She just didn't know if it would be enough.

Jamila handed Layla a cloth to wash her private parts as she readied herself to choose her future husband.

'You get to wear make-up today for the first time,' Jamila said.

'The second time,' Layla corrected.

'Ah, yes, you were wearing make-up that time you had a seizure.'

Layla turned at the slightly wry note in Jamila's voice and for the first time since she had returned to her family they shared a small smile. And then Layla's eyes filled with tears, because Mikael was right: she loved Jamila too.

Horrible, *horrible* love, Layla thought, hugging her handmaiden.

'Please come with me when I marry,' Layla begged.

'You know that I can't,' Jamila said. 'On your wedding day it will be my time to retire. Hussain will give you new maids and a new handmaiden. A young one who will help you with your babies.'

'I don't want babies,' Layla said, and then defiance crept back as Jamila helped her out of the bath. 'Anyway, who says that I am going to *choose* Hussain?'

'You will do the right thing by your father and

King, I am sure,' Jamila said as she started to pull out all the rags that had been put in Layla's hair the night before.

'Have you ever been in love, Jamila?' Layla asked.

'I have never been married.'

'Nor have I,' Layla said, but she had been in love—she *was* in love and for ever would be— and she did not want to be with another man.

'You are in a funny mood today, Layla,' Jamila observed.

'I don't feel funny,' she said as Trinity came in.

It was a dangerous mood she was in, and Jamila had every reason to be worried—for she knew that Layla was volatile at the best of times.

'Your hair's so curly,' Trinity said when she saw Layla. 'It looks wonderful.'

Layla said nothing, though her eyes glittered with suppressed rage as she forced a smile for Trinity.

'How is Zahid?' Layla asked.

Trinity swallowed. 'He is fine.'

'Does he send his best wishes for me today?'

Layla asked with spite in her voice, for she was so jealous of Trinity and Zahid, and so cross that the rules were different for them. 'Does he hope that my marriage will be as blessed and as happy as his? Because if he does he's a hypocrite—as are you.'

'Zahid loves you.'

'So many people who love me!' Layla shrugged. 'Aren't I lucky?'

Trinity was close to tears. Just knowing that Mikael was on his way and that Layla did not know had her heart racing.

Jamila painted Layla's eyelids and eyelashes till they glittered as much as the Opium ruby that she would hand to the man she chose.

'I wonder what gift Hussain will have for me,' Layla said. 'I doubt he will bring flowers.'

'You are to behave today,' Jamila said.

Layla swallowed down tears and then nodded, for she had promised that if she could just have her freedom for a short while then she would marry with dignity and grace.

Oh, it was *hard*, though.

'I shall do your lips and cheeks after you are in your robe,' Jamila said.

Layla stood and lifted her arms, and tried not to shake as the white and gold robe was slipped over her head.

She opened her eyes and saw Trinity was looking out of the window. And then she turned and stared at Layla, and there were tears in Trinity's eyes, and Layla could no longer be angry.

It was not Trinity's fault; it was just ancient rules that had to be obeyed.

Now was the time to be brave.

'I will be okay.' Layla smiled, for she loved Trinity, even if she was cross and so very scared. 'I always knew that this day would come.'

CHAPTER EIGHTEEN

MIKAEL GAVE HIS name at the palace gates and drove slowly forward when they opened.

He was nervous.

He had not lied to Layla that day in the café. Until she had come into his life he had never cared about anybody enough to be nervous.

Mikael drove through the gates and climbed out of the car. He looked up to the gleaming palace and saw a blonde-haired woman step back from a window.

So, Trinity knew that he was here.

A small door carved within the huge main ones opened and a robed man who did not introduce himself gestured for Mikael to follow him. He led him around the side of the palace and to another door.

From there he was taken through a labyrinth of

corridors to doors that had guards beside them. When they were opened, Mikael stepped in to face his judge and jury.

'It is customary to bow when you greet the King,' Fahid said. He sat at his desk and Zahid stood behind him, a little to the side.

Mikael bowed.

He could see the fury in the King's eyes and indeed Fahid *was* furious—for Zahid had just told him that Layla had possibly been friends with the man they had just paid. A man they had thought had taken care to ensure that Layla was safe and looked after.

Layla had told him herself that she had danced, and of other things that she had done.

'You are dismissed,' Fahid said to Abdul, and when it was just the three of them he addressed Mikael. 'I assume you are not here to discuss your fees?'

'That is correct,' Mikael said.

Ill, old, Fahid was still very much a king, and he looked with distaste at this man who came from a country with the most expensive apples in the world.

'Why are you here?' the King demanded. 'What is it you want?'

'Permission to ask Layla to be my wife.'

Mikael heard an angry breath from the King before he responded.

'A commoner does not ask royalty to marry him. It is for Layla to choose...'

The King halted then. He was an honest man, but as he met Mikael's eyes he looked away, for the truth was that Layla did *not* truly choose.

'I went through your bill very carefully and I also spoke with Layla. She says that she drank alcohol and danced. Were you with her when she did these things?'

Fahid did not give Mikael time to answer.

'The fact you are here must mean that something more went on in those days that she was away.' The King was almost shaking in fury. 'Or is she such an amazing dancer that you want to marry her? *Was* there a romance?' Fahid demanded.

Mikael looked briefly to Zahid. He was terrified now for Layla, for the damage his being here might cause her, but Zahid gave Mikael the slightest nod.

'Yes,' Mikael said. 'There was a romance.'

'Have you any idea how foolish of you it is to admit that?' The King stood. 'What went on between the two of you?' he demanded.

Mikael's face was as impassive as it was in court. He watched every flicker of the King's reaction as he used one of the few weapons he had against this powerful man.

'Your Highness, just as you must have the moment you saw Layla, I fell in love.' He watched as the King's hand moved to his ear. The slight telling gesture told Mikael he was right and so he continued. 'The first time I looked into her eyes I knew I would do anything to save and protect her.' He looked to Zahid, who stared straight ahead. 'I knew that Layla would do those things with or without me, and I considered her safer with me than without.'

'Oh, so you did *not* lead my daughter to do these

things? You are telling me that it was all Layla's fault…?' He cursed at Mikael, but Zahid spoke to his father in Arabic.

'Father, I realise now that Layla had been planning this escape for some time. She tried to go to London with me once. She would have done those things there.'

Fahid felt sick at the thought of Layla in London, trying those things, doing those things, and he looked to Mikael again, who had returned her with not so much as a bruise. Here was a man he begrudgingly admired for having the nerve to stand before him and admit to these things.

'Did she ask you to get her a joint?' Fahid asked.

'She did.'

'And you said no to her?'

The King frowned, for very few people said no to his daughter.

'Did she remind you she was a princess?' Fahid watched the slightest smile twitch on Mikael's lips.

'She did.'

'But still you said no.' Fahid thought for a

moment and then turned and spoke to his son in Arabic.

'I should have him removed.'

Very possibly he could have Mikael killed, Zahid guessed, for he doubted it had been such a sweet romance as the one Mikael depicted.

'You could pardon him for ensuring she returned safely,' Zahid said.

'King Fahid.' Mikael pulled out his final weapon. 'I understand you know nothing about me. And I cannot imagine raising a daughter alone, as you have done. It must be unbearable that your wife is not here to discuss this with—'

'There is nothing to discuss!' Fahid snapped.

But Mikael knew that the seed had been sown, for the King closed his eyes and breathed in for a moment, and it was as if Annan had stepped into the room to plead for their daughter's freedom. Mikael could see the struggle on Fahid's features as his once wild wife fought from the grave for her child.

The King spoke some more in Arabic to his son and Zahid translated his words to Mikael.

'My father says you are as arrogant as a rooster, and if you did marry her it would mean you would bow to him, obey him…' Zahid challenged.

'I would.'

Zahid crossed the room and walked till he was in Mikael's face. 'Given that one day I will be King, are you therefore saying you would also bow to *me* and obey?'

A muscle flickered in Mikael's cheek but he had planned his closing argument and was prepared.

'I will be more obedient to you than to my own right hand.'

Mikael watched the slight flare in Zahid's eyes as he answered him with an Arabic saying that might just mollify the King, but then Zahid closed his eyes in regret as Mikael qualified it slightly.

'When I am in Ishla.'

Zahid knew the King would never let Mikael take her away, as he was clearly hoping to do.

'If Layla moved to Australia I would do my best to give her a wonderful life and return here often. When here, I will wear robes and bow and do everything that is expected. It would be my pleasure to do so.'

'You will not take her overseas,' Fahid said.

'All I want is for Layla to be safe and happy—as must you.' He knew the King was ill, and yet he pushed on. 'I know how nervous she must make you, for I felt the same fear. She is independent and strong, and she insisted I leave her so she could enjoy her freedom, and yet...' He looked right at the King and both matched and voiced what was surely the King's greatest fear. 'I was scared at the thought of her in the world without me.'

'She is the end of the vine...' Fahid's voice wavered. 'My daughter, my precious. I don't want her overseas.' The King looked to his son and then back to Mikael. 'I am not just talking about tradition...'

'I understand that fear,' Mikael said. 'Your daughter is trouble. I wanted her off my hands, and yet I felt ill at the thought of her coping in a city she wasn't used to. If Layla came to live in Australia then I would take time off from work—

however long it takes—to ensure she understands all that your son does, having lived overseas. Layla could still work, still see her students...'

'I don't want to lose her.'

For the first time in more than two decades Zahid watched as his father struggled not to break down.

'You could never lose Layla,' Mikael said.

It was then that Mikael was glad that Trinity was not there. She did not understand just how ingrained these traditions were. She would have argued Layla's case, interrupted him; instead Mikael had stated his own case to a king who was listening.

'You couldn't lose Layla,' he reiterated, and then admitted what he perhaps shouldn't. 'I have already asked her to marry me and she laughed in my face. She said she would not turn her back on her country and you. I am as sure as I can be that Layla would only ever leave with your blessing— and, if she did, she would return often with love and gratitude to you.'

Mikael had nothing left. He had used every

argument he could, every weapon in his arsenal, had planned every move to the endgame.

It was as if the Queen that Layla so sorely missed had nudged him to checkmate.

Yes, it was for the King to decide now—but before he did, Mikael voiced the one united thought of everyone present in the room.

Even Queen Annan.

'I love Layla.'

CHAPTER NINETEEN

'READY?' TRINITY ASKED.

'I am,' Layla said, though her heart was breaking.

Of course she was ready, she told herself. She had known for ever that this day had to come.

'I have my memories and I have all my dreams…'

'You do.'

Trinity was torn. It was like taking a beautiful lamb to slaughter; how she wanted to tell Layla that Mikael was here, and yet Zahid had told her not to.

In this she had to trust that her husband knew best.

Layla walked down the palace stairs, determined to see this through without breaking down—and then she saw the closed doors and thought of the men behind it, and Hussain.

She looked down to her wrist, at the tiny little mark there, and knew that the match had burned more than twice for now it flared again.

'No!' Layla screamed, and went to run up the stairs.

Jamila grabbed her arms and a guard caught her by her dress as she dropped to the floor.

'She's having another seizure!' Jamila shouted. 'No!'

She kicked and she fought and Mikael, who was kneeling with the other suitors as the King sat on his throne, lowered his head and smiled as he heard her scream his name, weep and beg that she wanted to die a virgin spinster if she could just dream of him each night. It was the sound of torture, but it came from love.

Mikael lifted his head and looked to Hussain, who was kneeling to his right. It had to be him, for he was an arrogant and pompous git, but he was sweating now as he was shamed for a second time. Mikael felt another gaze on him then, and looked over into the tired eyes of the King as Layla's screams continued to fill the palace.

'Perhaps you can handle her?' the King said to Mikael.

Fahid was weary and, though he would never admit it, it was quite a relief that Mikael was here today—especially now, as Mikael stood and took over the rebel princess.

He would take care of her, Fahid knew, and he felt the first glimmer of peace as they walked out of the room to the spectacle that awaited. He loved his wild daughter so…

'Layla…' Mikael's fingers gripped her cheeks just in time to stop her biting a guard. 'It is time to choose your husband.'

Layla thought she was dreaming—for dressed in robes of white and gold, and just so beautiful, was the man who would for ever live in her dreams. Not a night had passed since their parting that hadn't been spent together in her mind.

'Mikael…' She stood for a sixth of a second, then leapt like a cat into his arms.

'Layla!' her father scolded as Mikael put her down. 'You are to follow tradition.'

'Father, I don't understand…' She frowned. She

could barely make sense of anything; she looked to her father and simply didn't understand how Mikael was here or what was going on.

'Mikael has spoken with Zahid and me today. He wants to give you a life in Australia but you shall return here often. It is up to you if you choose this man as your husband.'

'Oh, but I do.'

'Layla…' The King's tone warned her of their traditions. 'What do you do now?'

As she had on the day they had first met, she took the precious stone from her tunic and placed it down.

'You have to offer your gift to me now,' Layla said.

Trinity saved the day and retrieved Mikael's jacket from the room where he had changed into traditional robes.

'My wallet.' Mikael handed it over and smiled at the dark bastard he had once been, for he had sworn that if this day ever came there would be a watertight pre-nup; instead he handed her the keys to his home, his passport—she could have the lot.

'That's a black credit card,' he said as she went through his wallet.

'What's a credit card?' she asked.

'It means I can keep you in peeled, thinly sliced apples prepared by gourmet chefs.'

'Good.' Layla smiled.

Then she took out the folded piece of paper that told him she would never forget him, and the on-line chess name that she had thought might be their only link, and she looked up as Mikael spoke for the first time in Arabic. It was her favourite saying—one Layla had never thought could apply to the man who would be her husband

'Hayet albi enta,' Mikael said.

'And me.' Layla smiled again. 'You are the life of my heart too.'

CHAPTER TWENTY

MIKAEL BOUGHT A return flight this time, when he went back to Sydney without her.

There was an appeal to be lodged for his bastard client, and a lot of desk to be cleared—especially given that Mikael would be changing career direction when next he returned.

He poured a glass of sparkling water and even the bubbles seemed to fizz in delight as he acknowledged that when he returned it would be with Layla.

It was time to make a call.

'Demyan.' Mikael followed protocol. 'How is the baby?'

'Her name is Annika.'

'How is Annika?'

'She is awake for twenty-three hours a day,' Demyan said. 'I forgot how much noise babies make. So, where have you been? What happened with you and Layla?

'Well, as Layla would say, we are betrothed!'

Demyan laughed as he heard that Mikael would be getting married in Ishla and that it would be a very traditional wedding.

He'd laugh even more, Mikael thought privately, if he knew he was marrying a virgin. In fact Demyan might drop the phone if he found out that it was Mikael who had insisted that Layla save herself for their wedding night.

'Layla is going to be living here after we marry, but her father is not well so we shall be returning to Ishla often. I am not taking any more cases for now. I'm going to take a few months off to teach her about traffic lights and currency and such things.'

'You have it bad,' Demyan said, for he could hear the adoration in Mikael's voice even as he tried to keep it light.

'I have it so *good*,' Mikael said. 'Demyan, I understand it is short notice, and you have Annika, and things might be difficult to arrange, but—'

'We will be there.'

They had grown up on the streets together; they were family—just not by blood.

'Will you be part of the wedding party?' Mikael asked. 'You would have to frock up.'

Demyan said something very rude in Russian, and then laughed and said that he would be delighted.

'I need another favour,' Mikael said.

'Apart from my wearing a dress?' Demyan checked.

'I need to speak with Alina.'

'Alina?'

'Women's business.'

'Very well.'

It was possibly the most awkward conversation of Mikael's life, but for Layla he pushed through it.

'But, Father...'

They were waiting for Mikael to arrive back at the palace—not that Layla was allowed to see him till their wedding day. She was more excited than she had ever thought possible about her wedding, and yet it was dawning on her that she was moving far, far away.

'Jamila will be so bored without me, and she will fret and worry. I think it would be good for her if she came to live in Australia with me.'

'Jamila deserves to retire!' the King snapped.

'The car has just arrived!' Trinity walked in, smiling, and Layla started hopping on both legs.

'Five minutes?' she pleaded with her father. 'Please, can I just have five minutes alone with Mikael?'

'You will see him on your wedding day.'

'Please...' Layla begged. 'To know he is in the palace and not be allowed to see him is very cruel to me. Please...'

'Five minutes.' Her father gave a weary sigh. 'You,' he said to Trinity, 'go with her. And...' But then Fahid rolled his eyes What was the point? Trinity's chaperoning skills had got them to this place. 'Five minutes.'

Four were spent kissing, which left one minute to quickly take her contraband from Mikael's toiletries bag.

'You have no idea how hard it was to get these...'

Mikael rolled his eyes because, just as Layla had on her way to Australia, Mikael had had a little flutter of anxiety at Customs, wondering how he'd explain what he had in his bag.

Yes, he had packed it himself?

'I had to ask Alina to get them for you...'

'Are she and Demyan here.'

'Yes, and baby Annika. You will see them all at the wedding.'

He felt more than a touch uncomfortable, handing the packet of pills over, but Layla had insisted she wanted a perfect wedding night and had started retching when Mikael had tried to explain condoms. And she didn't want a baby just yet.

'You get twelve repeats.'

'Repeats?'

'Twelve months before you go to the doctor. Layla, I am fine if you decide that you do want a baby...'

'I don't want one yet.' She popped the shiny packet in her bra. 'So, a year of taking this every day and there'll be no baby—it's like magic...' She was ecstatic! 'We can party, we can swim, we can dance.' But then her face was serious. 'Thank you. This means a lot to me.'

Mikael knew she was scared about having a baby, and was just so grateful that he would be there for her if she ever wanted to address those fears.

Now, though, wasn't the time.

There was a wedding to get ready for.

Layla was far from the blushing bride.

She was glowing and smiling as she walked through the scented gardens on the arm of Fahid towards Mikael, who was dressed in gold robes and a headdress with Demyan and Zahid in silver beside him.

Trinity was in silver too, and Zahid remembered the last time she had been a bridesmaid as she walked towards him.

Demyan tried not to catch Alina's eye, because

she kept laughing at the sight of him in robes and head-gear.

Mikael saw no one except Layla.

Her dress was gold, and she had on a gold veil, and as she stood beside him Mikael saw that her eyelids had been painted gold too.

The first time he had seen Layla he had been reminded of the beauty of a new moon.

Now it felt as if the sun was stepping into his life.

It was a very short ceremony and there was no kissing the bride! The formal service was followed by a long meal, with laughter and love at the top of the menu and all the promise of the desert for the night.

As darkness descended Jamila handed Layla a goblet of liquid that should ensure their wedding night was a fertile one, and for the first time Layla's smile faltered.

Mikael watched her cheeks burn as she drank it down. She swallowed the drink and then looked to him, and she had never been more grateful for a person who understood her—a person she could be herself with and a wedding night that she did not fear now.

I feel guilty, her eyes told him.

It's fine, said his small smile.

As they went to leave and say their goodbyes again Layla's smile wavered as she embraced Jamila, and both women started crying.

'Thank you.' Mikael said it in Arabic to the old lady, and wished he could say more, but still Layla did not know that there had been a time when Jamila's love had been all she had had. 'Thank you for taking such good care of her.'

'Father, please!' The emotion of the day was catching up with her now, and at the thought of leaving Jamila behind Layla was crying. 'Why won't you let Jamila come to Australia with me…?'

For the last time the King stepped in.

'Layla, Jamila is staying here. You do not have to worry—she will be kept in splendour…'

'But I want her with *me*!'

'Well, you can't have her,' Fahid said. 'For Jamila has agreed to be my bride.'

There was a very stunned silence, followed by a shocked gasp from Layla.

Mikael dared not look at Demyan, for he knew his lips would be twitching—as were Mikael's.

Trinity smothered a laugh and Zahid closed his eyes as Fahid broke with tradition and in view of everyone kissed his future bride.

'Congratulations!' Alina beamed, delighted to see the couple looking so very happy and not comprehending what an incredible shock this was.

'We were going to wait till after the wedding,' Fahid explained. 'But you all have what you want, so why not us?'

'Congratulations.' Zahid spoke next, and even if his voice was a touch strained he was always polite, and he followed tradition and kissed Jamila's hand.

'Congratulations!' Trinity was more effusive, and she kissed not just Jamila's hand but the King's cheek too, for she had told him herself once that she hoped he would again find love.

'Congratulations,' Mikael offered, and Jamila raised her hand to him and he did as he had promised he would when in Ishla and followed tradition.

It was the Princess to his right, though, who was struggling with the news.

Layla felt Mikael's hand nudge the small of her back and she looked at Jamila, who gave her a nervous smile which she did not return.

As more congratulations were offered there were tears filling Jamila's eyes as still Layla stood rigid.

'This is *not* Planet Layla,' Mikael said in a very low voice, and his hand nudged the small of her back again.

'Congratulations,' Layla forced out through very tense lips, and then kissed Jamila's hand.

Fahid gave a small nod of gratitude to Mikael.

'I don't want to talk about it,' Layla said as she and Mikael headed to a helicopter, and she shook her head, as if to clear it from the unwelcome images dancing before her eyes. 'I don't even want to think about it.'

She let rip, though, when they were in the desert, in their tent and alone.

Mikael opened champagne as Layla stood swaying in stunned fury. 'He's marrying *Jamila*!'

'Layla…' Mikael warned.

'Has he lost his mind?' Layla said.

'Layla, he loves her.'

'My handmaiden—a *queen*!'

Mikael had heard enough.

'Layla, you will walk back into that palace happy for them,' he told her. 'Your father has done everything to ensure his children are happy—*everything…*'

He pointed his finger at her, and when she didn't smile, when she didn't make the biting noise she had on the day they had met, Mikael knew she was hurting inside.

'Now you ruin our wedding night,' she accused him.

She huffed off to the sleeping area and Mikael called to her.

'It won't work with me, Layla…'

He followed her in and was momentarily sidetracked, for he had never seen anything like it. There was nothing more luxurious than a desert sky at night, and with the tent's roof pulled back they would sleep under the stars in the vast marital bed.

'We are not married till we sleep together,' Layla said. 'You can still change your mind.'

'Nobody's talking about changing their mind, but your father deserves to be happy too.'

'What about my mother?' Layla asked. 'How long has this been going on?'

'That's none of our business.'

'Oh, but it is!' Layla roared. 'Has he forgotten his Queen?'

'Of course not,' Mikael said, and he took his bride in his arms and felt her heart racing as she struggled to process the news. He had guessed that it was this, not Jamila's lowly status, that was at the heart of her distress. 'Your father loves your mother and always will. I am quite sure of that.'

'How can you be?'

'When I tried to convince your father to allow you to marry me it was as if she was there in the room—talking to him, guiding him. Nothing will take their love away…'

The most cynical man in the world had confirmed what Layla felt in her heart—that her mother was somehow still there.

Layla thought about how happy she was and wanted everyone to feel the same—to feel as loved and as content and as excited about the future as she felt now.

'I am happy for Jamila and my father,' she said. 'I think it will be awkward, but I am going to try.'

'That's all you have to do.'

'Will you one day have forgotten *me*?' Layla asked.

'Never.'

'What if you hadn't come for me...?'

And there was her real fear—and it was scary even to voice it. But they had barely spoken since she had chosen Mikael and now, in his arms, she dared to face up to how terrible tonight might have been had it not been for Mikael.

'I was always coming for you,' he said to the shell of her ear. 'I'd have worked out your note, we'd have met online, I'd have lived in Ishla just to be near you...'

Mikael told her his truth—just not all of it, for he knew he would have appealed to Zahid on the death of the King and, whether she'd been married to another or not, he would one day have made Layla his.

'I would have spent the rest of my life either working out how to be with you or ensuring that you were happy.'

'What made you come when you did?'

'When I found out you loved me there was no question.'

'How could you not have known I loved you?' Layla frowned. 'Even if I could not say it, surely you knew…?' She pulled her head back and saw his eyes. He did not comprehend her words—but then how could he? Layla thought. For Mikael had never known love.

He would know it every day now.

It would not just be a year of dancing and kissing, Layla thought as her mouth moved to his. It would be a year of learning about a man who had never loved another—and what a privilege that would be.

Their first kiss as husband and wife was from another dimension, and knowing they did not have to halt, that they had the blessing of the desert, made it all the more sublime.

His chin was rough and it did not matter—for they were here in the desert for as long as they desired...and desire they did.

At every turn, in every intimate moment, Mikael had resisted—and now he did not have to.

Her tongue was the instigator, for it suckled his, and then she glimpsed Mikael without restraint. He was raising her robe and her hands lifted above her head, for she wanted it gone too.

She stripped, and so did he, and she stood as his mouth kissed her breasts till she could stand no more, and then they were side by side on the bed.

He tried to soften the mouth on her breasts but Layla pushed at his head in consent, for she had loathed how they had always had to hold back.

No more.

His mouth returned to hers and Layla was breathless—even more so as his hand slid between her thighs, stroking her clitoris as he swallowed the tiny shallow breaths that made Layla dizzy. And as his fingers slowly probed not even his kisses could temper the feel of him stretching her.

There would be no babies, Layla thought, for she could barely stand one finger…now two…

'It's okay,' he said to her grimace, and he was right.

His mouth was gentle balm as intimately he explored her, and soon it turned divine. Layla felt as if there were a key in the very small of her back that Mikael wound ever tighter with each deep stroke inside. Over and over he stroked, till the key was so taut she thought it might snap, but there was no fear.

Mikael wanted to ensure she was oiled and ready.

'Please…' Layla said, because she could not be more ready.

She was pulling him on top of her, for she wanted to be crushed by him—she wanted Mikael in the most basic of ways that till this moment they had had to deny.

She made an involuntary biting noise as she felt the first stretch of him and Mikael halted, but then he remembered that was what she did when she was over-excited. He waited for a moan, a protest—for anything that might indicate he should take it more slowly as for the first time he filled her—but Layla was lost in her own pleasure.

Mikael gave her a moment to acclimatise to the burning inside her body and she didn't know if her eyes were open or closed, for there were stars on either side.

'I like,' Layla said, and felt the soft shudder of his half-laugh. And then he started to move and she *still* liked.

He moved within her so slowly that she moaned in increasing want. She tasted salt on his neck and passion on his tongue and her hands pressed him in as her hips started to beg.

'I don't want to be a princess...'

It was a language of their own. She was not glass—and, though she loved that he treated her as such, in this moment there was no need to. There was just need.

He had accepted her password, Layla knew, because she felt this most guarded man unwind within her. He gave her himself and no longer held back, each thrust a shot of passion that drove her higher, wound her tighter, until that key was released and Layla's mind spun as her body concurred with Mikael's. Even her arms were trembling as he locked her into ecstasy and made her for ever his.

'Now you cannot change your mind,' Layla said as they came back to earth.

'I was never going to,' Mikael said, for he needed no get-out clause. He did not care about the small print of the contract they had entered into. 'Did I hurt you?' he asked, concerned he had not been gentle enough.

'Hurt me?' Her eyes widened. 'That is not hurt. Those nights I thought I had lost you—that was hurt...'

'You'll never lose me, Layla,' he said, and he meant it.

'I think we have to do this more than once a week.'

Mikael stared at the sky and the very full moon and held in his laughter before speaking. 'Once a *week*?'

'Jamila said that once a week would suffice. Can we do it more than that?'

'Absolutely.'

'How much more?'

'Much, much more.'

'What if those herbs make the pill not work?'

He looked over to her. 'I doubt that very much,' Mikael said, 'but what do you think would happen if it *didn't* work?'

She thought for a very long time about how she felt right now.

No, this wasn't Planet Layla, and yet since she had arrived on Planet Earth something had been missing.

There had been an ache.

She didn't really know what it had been, and now it was as if warm cement had been poured and that void was for ever filled. There was nothing she could not face with Mikael by her side.

'We'd get through it,' Layla said.

'We would,' he agreed, and he took her hand and she felt his fingers close around hers.

'I would probably be difficult to live with,' she warned, and Mikael rolled his eyes as he thought of life with a pregnant Layla.

'Yes, you would be *very* difficult to live with,' Mikael said, and then smiled as he thought about the day she had stepped into his chambers and claimed his black heart. 'But impossible to live without.'

'You say the nicest things.' She smiled. 'You are the nicest man.'

'Just make sure you don't tell anyone,' Mikael said, 'or you'll ruin my reputation.'

'It can be our secret,' she said, and then stamped her feet in pleasure and did a little horizontal dance in bed as happiness consumed her—for Layla knew she had met true love.

And Mikael watched on and let her be—delighted by his family.

* * * * *

MILLS & BOON®
Large Print – March 2015

A VIRGIN FOR HIS PRIZE
Lucy Monroe

THE VALQUEZ SEDUCTION
Melanie Milburne

PROTECTING THE DESERT PRINCESS
Carol Marinelli

ONE NIGHT WITH MORELLI
Kim Lawrence

TO DEFY A SHEIKH
Maisey Yates

THE RUSSIAN'S ACQUISITION
Dani Collins

THE TRUE KING OF DAHAAR
Tara Pammi

THE TWELVE DATES OF CHRISTMAS
Susan Meier

AT THE CHATEAU FOR CHRISTMAS
Rebecca Winters

A VERY SPECIAL HOLIDAY GIFT
Barbara Hannay

A NEW YEAR MARRIAGE PROPOSAL
Kate Hardy

0215 Rom LP

MILLS & BOON®
Large Print – April 2015

TAKEN OVER BY THE BILLIONAIRE
Miranda Lee

CHRISTMAS IN DA CONTI'S BED
Sharon Kendrick

HIS FOR REVENGE
Caitlin Crews

A RULE WORTH BREAKING
Maggie Cox

WHAT THE GREEK WANTS MOST
Maya Blake

THE MAGNATE'S MANIFESTO
Jennifer Hayward

TO CLAIM HIS HEIR BY CHRISTMAS
Victoria Parker

SNOWBOUND SURPRISE FOR THE BILLIONAIRE
Michelle Douglas

CHRISTMAS WHERE THEY BELONG
Marion Lennox

MEET ME UNDER THE MISTLETOE
Cara Colter

A DIAMOND IN HER STOCKING
Kandy Shepherd

MILLS & BOON®

Why shop at millsandboon.co.uk?

Each year, thousands of romance readers find their perfect read at millsandboon.co.uk. That's because we're passionate about bringing you the very best romantic fiction. Here are some of the advantages of shopping at www.millsandboon.co.uk:

* **Get new books first**—you'll be able to buy your favourite books one month before they hit the shops

* **Get exclusive discounts**—you'll also be able to buy our specially created monthly collections, with up to 50% off the RRP

* **Find your favourite authors**—latest news, interviews and new releases for all your favourite authors and series on our website, plus ideas for what to try next

* **Join in**—once you've bought your favourite books, don't forget to register with us to rate, review and join in the discussions

Visit **www.millsandboon.co.uk**
for all this and more today!